The Ghostly Victorians

(volume 1)

THE NOSTALGIA SERIES –
REVIVING THE PAST

Annette Siketa

Printed in the United Kingdom

First Printing, 2014 Alfie Dog Limited

The author can be found at: authors@alfiedog.com

Cover image: Alfie Dog Fiction

ISBN 978-1-909894-21-1

Published by
Alfie Dog Limited
Schilde Lodge, Tholthorpe,
North Yorkshire, YO61 1SN
Tel: 0207 193 33 90

DEDICATION

To Uncle Kevin. I didn't believe he was dead…until he told me.

CONTENTS

INTRODUCTION

At its zenith, the belief in ghosts in the Victorian era, bordered on the obsessional. From stately homes to deserted wells, no dwelling was complete without a resident ghost. Halls and mansions, and even the odd palace or two, spawned a multitude of family legends, many of which are still believed today.

Ghosts were true immortals, and had a greater presence than at any time in the past. Many people claimed direct contact with a spirit, whether verbally, or through a mediumistic object such as a Ouija board, or the use of a pen. Indeed, one private secretary allegedly continued to take dictation long after his employer was dead.

In books, plays, short stories and the like, love for the supernatural in the Victorian era was never more marked, and we can only speculate as to why. Perhaps fiction was the means of obtaining a vicarious thrill, after all, with nothing but drabness on the horizon, particularly those condemned to a life of servitude, happiness and contentment were as remote as the Antipodes. Imagination broke the barriers of belief, and through literature, perpetuated the existence of other worlds.

After the First World War, and subsequent increase in class consciousness, the existence of ghosts was greatly energized. No longer were they satisfied to silently slink around corners, or pop-up unexpectedly behind decrepit headstones. With their newly endowed rambunctiousness, even centuries old skeletons could do a little haunting. There was such an abundance of spooky creatures, that for the first time in its history, psychiatry became a profitable profession.

The era's contribution to science, exploration, and technology, was immense, and as any Victorian ghost will tell you, it did not do to fall behind. They became less simple and primitive than their ancestors, and instead of gliding to their haunting place, they took a bus or caught a train. Indeed, it was amazing how many of them learned to use a typewriter, or employed a palette to paint a picture of infinity. Their knowledge of 'modernisation' became so profound, that had they been able to return to the mortal world, they would have been geniuses.

This is not to suggest that as literature and social attitudes advanced, ghosts became less frightening. On the contrary, not only did it increase their level of influence, but their evil deeds as well. With their ability to instigate fear without a physical presence, writers such as Edgar Alan Poe, Algernon Blackwood, and even Sir Arthur Conan Doyle in his early works, created stories that both terrified and absorbed public imagination.

Victorian ghosts had an originality that their insipid forbearers lacked. For example, the man who returned from the grave to seek revenge – all those who looked into his eyes met their doom. Then there are the headless ghosts or those with missing limbs.

A surgeon whose desire to experiment in anatomy, is haunted to death by a needlessly amputated arm. Without doubt, such ability increased the level of horror, and when combined with other elements of the supernatural, it added impetus to the chill of fear.

In this collection, I have attempted to provide varying examples of individual stories. Yet in the final analysis, we are all as great as our daydreams…or our nightmares, so turn out the lamp, read this book by candlelight, and if a shadow happens to 'move' in the corner…don't call me!

Annette Siketa, Adelaide, July 2014.

1
THE PRICE OF INTERFERENCE

I.

I happened to be in London in 1887, when a procession to celebrate Queen Victoria's fiftieth anniversary as monarch, took place. By coincidence, I was in London ten years later when a similar extravaganza, this time to mark her Diamond Jubilee, was about to be held. Being wiser this time, for I had only glimpsed her on the previous occasion, I secured a good position on the corner of St James' Street and Pall Mall. There were two rows of people, crammed like sardines, in front of me, but being rather tall, I could easily see over their heads.

As the procession turned into Pall Mall from the St James' Street, the crowd behind me began to surge forward, so much so, that it was all I could do to keep my balance, let alone my place. The little man in front of me offered no resistance as, inch by inch, I was pushed into his narrow back.

"I'm sorry," I said sincerely, hanging onto my hat as the crowd suddenly increased in volubility, and I was irresistibly pushed forward. But, instead of colliding with the little man, he split down the middle from top to toe, so that half of him was on either side of me.

I had never seen anything like it in my life. Not even the most skilled carnival or circus performer, could have engineered such a feat. I was tempted to look around for a bevy of mirrors, but considering that I was enmeshed in a massive crowd, and that the Queen of England was about to pass by, the idea that the trick was some form of optical illusion, was simply not sustainable.

"Good grief, what are you?"

"Get back you Yankee cur! I need to join together again." His accent was pure cockney, which probably accounted for his colourful clothes – brown trousers, a vivid green jacket, and an excessively bright floral waistcoat.

"I can't," I shouted above the now cheering din, "the crowd…"

"Sorry be hanged," he roared. "I'll show you what interference is, and you won't like it." A second later he was gone, and the awful truth hit me like a club. He was a ghost.

I was rescued from my stupefaction by a tremendous roar. I looked up just in time to see Her Majesty passing in her carriage. She was wearing a bonnet and hiding behind a parasol, so that only the lower half of her face was visible. Given the way her mouth was drooping, she was clearly not enjoying her parade. Quite frankly, it made me wonder why she'd bothered.

In every respect, the exercise was a colossal waste of time. Despondent, I returned to my hotel, ate a sombre dinner, and retired to my room. The little man was waiting.

Naturally I ordered him out, but no amount of pleading or cajoling, argument or reason, would induce him to leave. He talked for hours, and was vulgar in both speech and manners. At one point, I threw a book at him, but it was like trying to hit smoke, and by four o'clock in the morning, I'd had enough.

"If you won't go away, then I will."

"Go where you like, it won't do you any good. Yesterday was the 22nd of June. I shall keep interfering for exactly one year."

"Nonsense. Besides, I will be returning to America soon, so I will be out of your reach."

The awful creature sniggered. "You silly yank. I can go to America any time I like. I can lounge around unobtrusively on a steamer, but they tend to be a little slow. The quickest method, is to be blown across the Atlantic on a strong breeze, though they are not always reliable. One time I was aiming for New York, and ended up in Africa."

I rammed my hat onto my head and prepared to leave the room. "Then go blow yourself somewhere else, preferably up!"

"Idiot," he retorted. "You can't kill a ghost."

I wandered around for about three or four hours. Having never been up this early in London, it was extraordinary to watch the great metropolis coming to life. It was a strange kind of chaotic order, in that all the trades' people were dashing about and shouting instructions, yet such was the obvious normality of the practise, that there were next to no mishaps. Somehow, this stability quietened my mind, and by the time dawn broke in earnest, the sight of all those barrows and carts loaded with produce made me realise how hungry I was.

I generally eat very little first thing in the morning, but my appetite was as such, that nothing short of a full English breakfast would satisfy me. It was therefore with lighter mind and grumbling stomach, that I made my way to the Savoy.

My new-found confidence was given a further boost, when I saw, sitting at a private table next to a window, two persons whose acquaintance I had made on the steamer coming to England. Mrs Lowenstein was a typical American mother, with immovable opinions and a firm grip on righteousness. Her daughter Ellen, as might be expected, was as beautiful as she was haughty.

Having been invited to join them, which I did with alacrity, I had just speared a particularly nice piece of melon with a fork, when who should appear but the spectre. I think it is safe to say, that no man had ever entered the prestigious Savoy breakfast room, dressed in a pair of checked trousers that were loud enough to wake the dead, a green plaid waistcoat that would have been an indictable offence on any golf course, and an Ascot top-hat perched jauntily on the head.

"Hello old chap," he greeted, and slapped me on the back with such calculated force, that it sent the piece of melon flying off the fork. It landed in Mrs Lowenstein's cup of tea. Any notion that only I could see him, was instantly dispelled when he said, "Introduce me to your charming friends." He winked and gave Ellen a low-born smirk.

I was not surprised when Mrs Lowenstein stood up and said coldly, "Come along, Ellen, we will leave these gentlemen to their breakfast."

The horrid man sat down in Ellen's chair and began to devour her bread roll. "Not a bad piece of interference if I say so myself."

"Now see here," I began, but he broke off a piece of bread and threw it in my face.

"And yet not quite satisfying. I don't think you've learned your lesson yet. Yes, quite definitely, another dose of interference is called for," and on that ominous note, he vanished.

My appetite vanished with him, for Mrs Lowenstein was rather an influential figure in New York. Somehow, I must repair the damage. Accordingly, I sought a bell-boy, scribbled an apology on a card, and sent it up. Mrs Lowenstein's response, delivered verbally by the buttons, was immediate and unmistakable. "The lady said she's going out and will not return any time soon." Not even the Queen could have delivered a better snub.

I was so maddened, that I resolved to return to America at once. I left the Savoy, and sought the office of the White Star Line, where I booked a single room on the Majestic, sailing out of Liverpool the following morning.

I returned to my hotel, and was not surprised to find the little man waiting for me. In fact, I was rather counting on it. In anticipation that he could not resist gloating, I had already concocted a story.

"Going somewhere?" he asked as I packed.

"Yes. I have been invited to Brighton to stay with an old friend of mine, Mr Thomas Wilson. Perhaps you've heard of him?"

"No, but thanks for the address. Rest assured, I will not neglect you during your stay. Ta-ta for now."

I chuckled softly as I took the train to Liverpool, where the next morning, I embarked on the Majestic for New York.

II.

I stood at the bow and watched the huge anchor being raised. Very soon, a vast ocean would roll between me and the damnable spook. With a sense of relief, and escorted by a steward, I went to my cabin below stairs, whistling merrily as we traversed the corridors.

As we drew near to my cabin I heard an avalanche of

profanity issuing from within. There was condemnation of the soap, there was perdition for the lighting, there were maledictions upon the position of the porthole, and the bedding was incontrovertibly excommunicated.

"I don't believe it!"

"Sir?"

I looked at the steward. "Can't you hear it?"

"Hear what?"

"Him!" I said heatedly, almost tearing my hair out. "That interfering spook inside the cabin."

The steward straightened his starched white jacket, his expression wary and nervous. His eyes flickered over my shoulder for a moment, as though he were seeking reinforcements, and then he opened the door and stepped inside. "It is empty," he proclaimed, but of course, it was not. The ghost was sitting on my suitcase.

"Hello again," he said cheerfully. "Oh, don't worry, he can't see me. I can only be seen if I want to be."

Not trusting the blighter to keep his word, I tipped the steward handsomely and quickly ushered him out. "What are you doing here?" I asked when the door was closed.

"Taking a voyage, just like you."

"But I'm not taking a voyage. Once we've cleared the shipping channel, I'm going to jump overboard and swim to France."

"Humph…I'd rather drive a cab, as I used to do."

"So, that's what you were. It certainly explains your intelligence, after all, it takes a keen brain and high intellect to drive a cab from one end of London to the other." I had hoped my remarks about his former profession, would have made him angry enough to leave. When he didn't, I changed tack. "Would you like a drink?"

"No thanks, I don't indulge. But, let me offer you something in return." He reached into his jacket and withdrew two fine cigars. However, when I tried to bite off the end of mine I bit my tongue instead. He roared with laughter. "That's a ghost cigar, mortals can't touch 'em."

All thought of conciliation vanished. "You are a low-born swine," I shouted, "and if you don't get out of here right now, I'll break every bone in your body."

"Very well," he answered coolly, and picking up a nearby pad and pencil, began to scribble. "Here's the address."

"What address?"

"The address of the cemetery where my bones are buried. You go in by the side gate…"

"Get out! This is my cabin! I booked it, I paid for it, and I intend to have it."

With his own ghostly cigar dangling from his mouth, he jumped to his feet and began to clap. "Bravo! What a performance! You could play King Lear."

I lost all self-control. I picked up a water-jug and hurled it across the room. It passed straight through him and struck the mirror over the wash-stand. As the shattered pieces fell to the floor, the door to the cabin slowly opened and three men stood in the doorway - the Captain, the steward, and a stern looking man, whose expression proclaimed that this was not a social visit.

"What's all this about?" said the Captain stiffly.

"I engaged this cabin for myself alone," I said, my voice shaking with rage, "and I object to his presence." I pointed to the spot where the little man was now grinning indecently.

"What presence?" demanded the Captain, following

my finger but clearly seeing nothing.

"Why him! The ghost, the spook, whatever you want to call it. He's settled in my cabin, and damn it, Captain, I won't stand for it."

The Captain sighed and addressed the other man. "Have you a strait-jacket?"

"It's certainly what he needs," I said through clenched teeth. "But it won't do any good. I don't think you can fit a ghost into a strait-jacket."

The other man stepped forward and gently took my arm. "I am a Doctor. Come and lie down, you obviously need peace and rest."

"Who - me? Not by a long shot. Just get him out, that's all I ask."

"Take off your clothes and get into bed," said the Doctor sternly. He turned to the Captain and whispered, "I need two of your strongest men. He's going to be trouble. Mad as a hatter."

What followed was a nightmare. I was forcibly unclad, had two yellow tablets rammed down my throat, and then strapped into my bed. It is a terrible condition to be sane, healthy, and full of life, only to be treated unjustly because of a beastly cockney ghost.

I continued to howl my sentiments, and on the second day out from Liverpool, the two maiden ladies in the cabin next door, made representations to the Captain, stating in the most emphatic terms, that they could no longer endure the shrieks of a maniac. Shortly thereafter, I found myself strapped in a cot in the steerage section, and it was not long before my spiritual persecutor materialised.

"What on earth are you doing there?" he asked in feigned surprise, sitting on the edge of the cot.

"Very funny," I said contemptuously. "When I die and become a ghost, I will seek you out, and by thunder, give you a thrashing you'll never forget." He seemed to pale at this, but I was too tired to gloat over such a minor victory.

I would never classify myself as an actor, but I realised that if I wanted to get out of there, I would need to act rationally. The ruse worked, and a few days later, I was released. Except for those occasions when I caught a member of the crew spying on me, I went about, and eventually disembarked, unhindered.

III.

Somewhat curiously, I did not see my spook again until November. I had been invited by a college to give a lecture on poetry, but such were his guffaws, rude noises, and cat-calls, that I could not continue and left the platform. It was then that I decided to consult an old friend of mine, Martin Peters, who specialised in paranormal psychology.

We met for dinner at a club where, over the port and cigars, I explained my predicament. "So you see, the man is ruining my life. Mrs Lowenstein has made me a social outcast, the Captain of the Majestic doubts my sanity, and now for the first time in my life, before some two thousand people, I break down in a lecture that I have delivered dozens of times. It cannot go on."

"I should say not," said Peters. "I might be able to help you get rid of him, but I'm not positive about it, for my new scheme isn't perfected yet. Have you tried the fire-extinguisher method? I've employed it twice before, and successfully. Fire is the vital essence of all these chaps. If you can turn the nozzle of your extinguisher on him, he will simply 'go out'."

Buoyed by his encouragement, I returned home determined to try it. Prudence dictated that I should practise first, so I retrieved my extinguisher, set a small spirit fire in the rear yard, and depressed the nozzle. When the fire went off like a fountain loaded with dynamite, I let out a cry of joy. At long last, I had an answer.

Sadly, it was not to be. Somehow, the obnoxious creature had discovered the plan, for when he came to my house later that night he was amply protected from the annihilating liquid. He was wearing a mackintosh and a black felt hat, both of which were glowing like coals, though no material object was scorched or burned.

The only effect of the experiment was the drenching of a pile of manuscripts on my desk. Laugh? He was convulsive, rising into the air and tumbling like a barrel.

"Delightful," he cried. "Have you got another extinguisher?"

IV.

He returned some three weeks later. "I have come to apologise for making you ruin your work."

"It's a little late to be sorry. If you are sincere, then you'll go away and never darken my doorstep again."

"Ah, no, my friend. That is not possible yet. However, I have corrected the damage."

I had a horrible sense of foreboding. "What have you done?"

"I have re-written your work."

"You…you've done what?" I cried.

"It seemed only fair that I should write it again, so I've sent to your regular editors, half a dozen poems and short stories in your name. The sonnet to a coal bucket was the longest of all. I think it will take up about six magazine pages."

Somewhat stupidly, I started to argue. "But a sonnet never contains more than fourteen lines."

"It does now. This new one of yours has over 400. Then there's the three-page quatrain on immortality that I sent to, 'The Methodist Magazine'. If I say so myself, it's the funniest thing I've ever read." He produced one of his accursed cigars, but could hardly light it for laughing. "And you'll get all the credit. Goodbye for now."

He left me in the deepest despair I had ever experienced. Not content with ruining me socially – though my aspirations in this regard were never very high, he had attacked me where it would hurt the most, my literary reputation. I could only hope that somehow, he had made a mistake, or that my editors would realise that it was not my writing.

But, as the steady stream of returned manuscripts showed, it was not to be. Though he had copied my style exactly, there is no word in any language, no matter how primitive or impolite, to accurately describe the substance of the pages. Every editor, some of whom I had known for years, suggested that I stop writing for a while. One even intimated that I should seek professional help.

Angry and frustrated, with a cry like a wounded animal, I picked up an ink-bottle and hurled it at the wall.

V.

I put on my hat and hurried to the telegraph office, where I despatched an urgent message to Peters.

'Is your new method perfected yet? If so, please bring here at once. Need help badly. Answer collect'.

My agitation was not helped by his flippant response.

'I don't know why you wish me to answer collect, but I suppose you have your reasons. So I answer as you request: collect'.

It was a mean telegram to send to a man in such an unhappy state. I was sitting at my desk composing a hot retort, when the bothersome spook showed up.

"Well, what do you think of my, or should I say, your literary work?" He sat back on the couch as though he owned it, his piggy eyes examining the ink-spots on the wall. "Novel design that. You ought to apply to a wallpaper company for a job. Given an accurate aim and plenty of ink, you can't be beaten for your splatter work." I ignored him. "Sulky, eh? You shouldn't brood you know. Impotent wrath can be very destructive. I once had a passenger who hired my cab to drive him around London. We stopped at a chop-house where he asked me to wait. He never came back. Left by the back door. Well, I mean, what's an honest cabbie to do? Naturally I searched for the blighter, but never found him. Then, three years after I died, I saw him, and pursued him everywhere in my phantom cab. When he went to church, I drove the cab up the aisle. When he called on a friend, I parked the cab in the parlour, the horse stamping and whinnying like a banshee. Of course, only he could see it. Lord, how mad he was. He finally burst like a bubble. It was most amusing. Even the horse laughed."

I finally looked up. "How much was the fare?"

"Five bob."

I slowly put down my pen. "So, you murdered a man for the sake of five shillings. How little you value life."

The little man jumped to his feet. "Murder! I never killed anyone in my life."

"Oh yes you did. You just told me that you drove this

man to his death. That, my friend, is murder. Jokes and tricks are fine in their proper place, but when they turn deadly, they are no longer funny, and you are the least amusing individual I have ever met. Now, get out."

Afterwards, when I analysed the conversation, for I had unconsciously written it down, I couldn't believe how calm I had been. Moreover, my accusation had caused him distress. Was this a 'chink' in his seemingly impenetrable armour? Did they have rules & regulations in his realm, and by exposing his murderous past, he had broken one? I went to bed pondering these hypotheses, and awoke the next morning to find Peters on my doorstep.

"What are you doing here?" I asked grumpily.

"Your telegram of course."

"I didn't think much of your reply."

"My reply? But it was perfectly clear."

I groaned and produced the missive. "I think my spectre has been interfering again."

Peters stared at the telegram in disbelief. "I didn't write this. My reply was that I would be here tomorrow with a new idea for getting rid of your problem."

"Sorry," I said, abashed.

Peters crumpled the telegram and threw it in the fire. "Right," he said with determination, "I need to inspect your heating arrangements."

"What on earth for?"

"Did you ever notice, when smoking in a room that is heated by a furnace, how the smoke gets caught in its draught?"

"Yes, what of it?"

"The smoke is twisted until it gets free, or is torn apart. I was conducting some experiments the other day, nothing to do with your situation, but as I watched the smoke rise and then be dispersed by my furnace, the solution to your problem came to me. I remembered that you had a furnace and a fire, so all you have to do is get the obnoxious spook in the right position, and turn a blast from the furnace on him."

"By Jove! You are a genius!"

I shook his hand so vigorously, that he was forced to remonstrate. "Save your energy for him, you'll need it. Make no mistake it will not be pleasant to witness."

I shuddered as I thought of the plan, and for a moment, was inclined to reject the offer. But my weakness evaporated when I recalled the harm he had unjustly inflicted – the embarrassment, the humiliation, the potential ruin of my career, and of the poor man driven to his death.

Peters and I began to experiment, calculating distances for maximum impact. We then tested the capacity of the furnace using soap bubbles. The results were most gratifying. The shapes that formed as they were blown about the room before finally bursting, were truly wonderful.

To my great annoyance, it was two weeks before he showed up again. However, my mood was tempered due to the fact that it was extremely cold and blowing a gale, ideal conditions for setting the trap. The fire was lit, and the moment he materialised, I surreptitiously closed the vents on the furnace.

"Oh, you're back," I said nonchalantly.

"Did you miss me?"

"As a matter of fact, I did." He looked at me suspiciously, but I was expecting this. "Now that I know there's no escape for me, I don't seem to feel so bad. How have you been?"

"Bah…you know full well that you don't like me. What game are you playing?"

"Well," I slowly began, pretending to hesitate, "I was wondering if you would tell me more of your adventures as a spirit. If I am to be persecuted by a ghost, the least I can do is immortalise him in a book."

"A book? You want to put me in a book?"

I had no intention of immortalising the horrid little man. In truth, I was stalling. I needed the room to cool down so I could get him in front of the furnace. With the plummeting temperature outside, it would not take long.

"Of course," I said convincingly. "Would you like a drink?"

"Would you like a cigar?"

I wagged a finger at him. "No thanks." I moved behind my desk, picked up my pen, and looked at him inquiringly.

He lay on the couch, clasped his hands behind his head, and began, "I was born in London, Marylebone to be exact. My mother…" He spoke for almost an hour, but I only made desultory notes. It had to look convincing. Then finally, he said the words I most wanted to hear. "Brr…it's cold in here."

"So sit by the fire," I said in an absent voice, pretending to read the notes.

From the corner of my eye, I saw him look at the fireplace with mistrust. "Ha! You don't fool me that easily. No doubt you've prepared a log packed with explosives."

I genuinely laughed, for the idea had never occurred to me. "How suspicious you are."

"Yes, I always am of suspicious characters," he replied, getting off the couch and planting himself in front of the furnace. By acting contrary to my suggestion, he probably thought it would annoy me. I waited. "There isn't any heat here," he said.

"No heat? Damn, I forgot to turn it on." It was the longest ten feet I will ever walk. I went to the furnace and opened the vents.

He was caught in the current, and like the soap-bubbles, was pulled into the most fantastic shapes. But seconds later, the current blew him across the room directly towards the fireplace. Toes first, he started to float up the chimney, laughing uproariously at the ease of his escape.

I could do nothing but watch on helplessly. A lifetime of misery flashed before my eyes. Then, oh glorious relief, a back draft caused by the howling wind, blew him back into the room again.

Kicking and swearing, his struggling reminded me of the time I had been confined to the straight-jacket. It was the only moment when I felt any sympathy for him.

"Lemme down! Lemme down!" he screeched, as his body assumed grotesque attitudes. Then, one by one, his limbs began to stretch like elastic, until eventually they snapped off and floated up the chimney.

Silence, complete and utter silence. It had only taken minutes, yet it had felt much longer, and I was too stunned to laugh over my triumph. Somehow, I had the presence of mind to turn off the furnace before going to bed. When I awoke next morning, I was still fully clothed.

I could not face breakfast, so went to the telegraph office. My message to Peters said simply, *'It worked'*.

The curious thing is that my cockney spectre did achieve a sort of immortality. Once I had recovered my wits, I found the notes I'd made, and using them as a base, created a series of children's books entitled, Mr Spook. I received some compensation for the outrages I had suffered as the books were very popular.

2
SEASIDE & SPIRITS

Due to a persistent foot injury and nagging cough, my physician advised that I should exchange, albeit temporarily, the grimy and soot-laden metropolis, for the efficacy of fresh salty air. Accordingly, I rented a house in the romantically named Smugglers Cove. It was a small but thriving fishing community, yet even after I had explained this to my two young sons, their excitement at the prospect of pirates and buried treasure, was not diminished. With adequate railway services to hand, the upheaval from city to shore was, I am happy to say, uneventful.

The house faced the sea, and was one in a row of six. It had a small garden in the front, a coach-house and stable in the rear, and between these buildings and the house itself, a considerable expanse of lawn. The rooms, though not overly large, were well-maintained and comfortable. Moreover, to judge from the lingering odour, the interior had recently been painted.

My 'entourage' consisted of my wife, Annabelle, my sons James and Thomas, otherwise known as Jamie and Tommy, aged 9 and 7 respectively, their nanny, Miss Sutherland, the cook, Mrs Greenwood, the housemaid, Ellen Faith, and my estimable butler, Roxon. I had been advised that an old woman, named Mary Pickles, was the caretaker, but that she would vacate the premises prior to our arrival.

The servants and luggage having preceded us,

everything was, more or less, ready for our arrival. The only sour note was the weather. A howling wind was battering the coast, so that the roaring fire in the drawing-room hearth, and the pervasive smell of Mrs Greenwood's excellent cooking, were welcome in the extreme. The weather notwithstanding, the house was cosy and cheerful, and highly conducive to pleasant anticipation.

We were all exhausted from the rigours of the day, so after a hearty dinner, everyone settled down for their first night in the house. Miss Sutherland had packed the children off to bed hours earlier. A small but adequate room on the first floor had been designated as the nursery. The master bedroom, with its four-poster bed and dark heavy hangings, was also on this floor.

Mrs Greenwood had been ensconced in a small room off the kitchen. Truth to tell, it was little bigger than a pantry, but, as she stoutly declared after rejecting more spacious accommodation on the second floor, "I'll not desert me stove." Roxon and Emily had made no such objections, however, I did think Roxon was a little 'put out'. Unlike our home in London, there were now two flights of stairs between him and the kitchen.

With candle in hand, Annabelle and I climbed the stairs to our bedroom. Through the open doorway I could see Ellen's shadow crossing the ceiling as she moved about the room.

"Listen to that wind," said Annabelle with a violent shiver, the flame of her candle spluttering. "There must be a draught."

As most of the windows facing the sea were rattling slightly I laughed at her foolishness. "My dear wife, I doubt there's a house along the coast that doesn't have at least one good draught."

"Did you…" but before she could finish, there was a high-pitched scream from our bedroom.

We darted up the remaining stairs. Ellen was standing just inside the door, her back pressed onto the wall. I had never seen anyone look so frightened.

"What is it?" I demanded. When she didn't answer, I had to shake her. "What is it?" I repeated.

Ellen pointed to the bed. "A man," she trembled, her lips white with shock. "A big man."

"What happened, Ellen," said Annabelle softly, taking the girl by the hand and leading her to a chair.

"I was turning down the bed, when from the corner of my eye, I saw a very tall man standing beside me."

"What did he look like?" I asked between coughs, for although the bedroom fire was low, there was a cloud of smoke hanging in the air. But, it was beyond Ellen's comprehension to provide a decent description, other than to say that he was 'dressed in black'.

We both endeavoured to reassure her, and after a restorative nip of brandy, Annabelle escorted Ellen to her room. I was already in bed when she returned.

"Poor thing, she'll probably have nightmares for days. I wonder what could have frightened her like that."

"This," I said, tugging the nearest bed hanging. "Look at the colour. It's so brown as to be almost black, and have you noticed the amount of smoke in the room? It was obviously blown back down the chimney by the wind. Put the two together, couple it with exhaustion and the dim light, and what have you got?"

The incident was quickly forgotten, though Ellen was rather skittish from that point on. Then, about a week later, Annabelle and I were having breakfast in the dining-room, when Roxon entered with a pot of tea. He began to clear some of the dishes, but as he did so, he looked at me directly and jerked his head towards the door. When I frowned, he looked at my wife and shook his head.

More curious than alarmed at his strange behaviour, I made an excuse and went into the yard, Roxon close on my heels. Before either could say a word however, Jamie and Tommy came tearing out of the house, their faces beaming with excitement.

"Daddy," panted Jamie, "we're going to the beach to dig for buried treasure." They had been doing this every morning since we'd arrived, which was probably why Miss Sutherland was looking rather jaded. She had clearly underestimated the adventurous spirit of two curious boys.

"I do apologise for my behaviour, sir," said Roxon when we were alone, "but what I have to say is for your ears only."

"I gathered that," I said dryly. "Go on."

"Last evening, I was lying in bed and looking at the moon, when I saw a strange light reflected in the window."

"You mean it was something outside?"

Roxon shook his head solemnly. "No, sir. It was inside my room. I turned my head, and saw the figure of an old woman rummaging around on the floor."

"An old woman? Are you sure?"

"Oh, yes sir. She had her back to me, so naturally I couldn't see her face, but there was enough moonlight to see that her shawl and bonnet were quite ragged. I was about to call out when she..." He broke off, clearly uncomfortable with the recollection.

"It's alright, Roxon. You know you can tell me anything."

Seemingly reassured, he went on, "The thing is, sir, when she turned around, she appeared to be holding a flaming red coal." He paused as though anticipating a reaction, but if this were so, it was a pointless gesture for I had no idea what to say. "I saw her face by the light," he continued. "It was, I'm sorry to say, quite hideous. Her face was deeply pitted with the scars of smallpox, and there was a disturbing cast in her right eye. I think it was blind."

I cleared my throat. "I have no desire to cast aspersions on your testimony, but are you sure you weren't dreaming?"

"I must admit that I thought that at first, but when I told Mrs Greenwood about it this morning, she almost dropped the frying pan. You see, she's also seen the woman."

"She hasn't mentioned it to me. When did she see her?"

"A few nights ago. She chased the woman into the coal-house, but when she arrived seconds later, the woman had disappeared."

"Is it possible," I said thoughtfully, "that it was Mary Pickles? This house is not exactly a mansion, and this area is not called Smugglers Cove for nothing. If there are any secret passages, then being a resident, Mary Pickles is bound to know about them." Judging from Roxon's pained expression, this thought had not occurred to him. I relieved his anxiety. "Leave it for a few days. If the woman shows up again, try and follow her, or better yet, find out who she is. I'll have a private word with Mrs Greenwood."

The matter was left in abeyance, but over the next few weeks, Roxon and Mrs Greenwood reported further sightings of the woman. Unfortunately, she was always, or so it seemed, too quick for them, disappearing around a door or dashing into the yard. She never spoke or looked at them, nor did she inflict injury or harm. Indeed, Mrs Greenwood expressed her surprise that, although the woman was, "In want of a good meal," no food was taken from the kitchen.

One morning, I was absently gazing out of the drawing-room window, when a woman matching Roxon's description, walked past the house. Cursing my injured foot, I rang the bell and waited impatiently. Roxon soon gave chase, but returned about ten minutes later, hot and panting and utterly dejected.

I had hired a local man, Watkins, to oversee the stables and my horse, Matilda. Shortly after Roxon's disastrous attempt at amateur detecting, I was approaching the stables intending to take a ride, when the sound of a commotion reached my ears.

"I don't know what's the matter with her, sir," said Watkins, trying to calm the jittery sweating horse. "Every time I try to put her into a particular stall, she baulks. She snorts and rears and will not set a hoof in it." This was out of character, for Matilda was ordinarily docile.

"Maybe she's frightened of the old woman," said Jamie, who was now standing beside me and eating an apple.

"She's ugly," said Tommy, who, having finished his apple, was holding out the core for the horse.

"Stand back lads," said Watkins in a warning tone. Matilda had shown every sign of rearing. I immediately pulled my sons away.

"Boys," I said, steadying my nerve, "what woman?"

"The one who keeps coming into the yard," said Jamie.

"She always searches in front of the stables," said Tommy. "I've asked her several times if we could help, but she always ignores me."

I looked at the lane at the rear of the property. The only access into my yard, was via a six foot high, heavy iron gate, which for the children's sake, was always kept locked. "How many times have you seen her?"

"About four or five," said Jamie. "She always comes in when Miss Sutherland is not present."

"We first saw her the morning after we arrived," said Tommy brightly, eager to have his say in the conversation.

"Has she ever spoken to either of you?"

"No," said Jamie. "She doesn't seem to notice us."

I sent the boys into the kitchen in search of a biscuit, and then turned my attention to Watkins. He had walked Matilda around the yard, and although she seemed calmer, there was still a nervousness in her movements.

"Have you seen this old woman, Watkins?"

"Only the back of her, sir. Beats me how she's getting in."

"Could it be Mary Pickles?"

"Nah." His tone was emphatic. "I know Mary Pickles, she's a good honest woman, and I can tell you now, sir, it ain't her." Alarming though this was, 24 hours later, I was given even greater cause for concern.

After breakfast, I went for a walk instead of a ride. It was a glorious day, and although I still needed the use of a cane, my foot was definitely on the mend. I returned home to an extraordinary sight. Jamie and Miss Sutherland were tussling at the top of the stairs.

"Daddy!" He broke away and ran down the stairs, his little face angry and pink. "Daddy, I'm not lying. Miss Sutherland says I am, but I'm not. I did see him!"

"Calm down, Jamie," I said in a cajoling voice, concerned that his face was now cherry-red.

Like a 'grande dame', Miss Sutherland descended the stairs, her hand resting lightly on the banister. "He's been dreaming, sir, a nightmare, no doubt caused by that awful incident yesterday with the horse."

"It wasn't a nightmare," said Jamie in a distressed voice, clinging to my trousers like a limpet.

I disentangled his arms, just as Miss Sutherland attempted to drag him away. She had cared for the boys for the past three years. She was firm, but kind, and I had never found cause for castigation. Yet there was something in her authoritative manner which, quite frankly, annoyed me.

"Leave him!" I took Jamie into the drawing-room, and gradually, the story came out.

He had been awakened during the night by the sound of the nursery door being opened. Thinking it Miss Sutherland, he was about to call out when he realised it was somebody else, somebody he had never seen before. Although the lamp was on a low wick, it was enough to see that it was a very tall man, dressed as Jamie described it, in old-fashioned clothes – a frock coat with the collar turned up, wide rough trousers like those of a sailor, and a pair of worn boots covered in mud.

The man stood beside the nanny's bed for a minute, which was next to the door. Satisfied that she was asleep, he moved across to the fireplace on the opposite wall, where he paused to stare into its dying depths. He then went to the dressing-table under the window, where he stood for a full two minutes, lightly running his fingers over the items laid on top.

Naturally, Jamie watched the proceedings in abject

terror, and when the man suddenly turned around, he pulled the covers over his head and lay like a block of ice. The next sound he heard, was the nursery door being softly closed.

Even though Tommy had remained asleep throughout the entire ordeal, and therefore unable to offer any corroboration, I did not doubt the veracity of Jamie's story, for the detail was too exact. This, coupled with the encounters experienced by Ellen and Roxon, could only point to one conclusion. Somehow, strangers were gaining access to the house.

Annabelle was out, and I didn't think Miss Sutherland would be in receptive mood. I therefore settled Jamie in the kitchen. Having briefly explained the situation to Mrs Greenwood, she clucked and fussed like a mother hen, while Roxon, Watkins, and I, made a thorough search of the house. We examined doors, we tapped on walls, we even removed the fuel from the coal-house, but nothing was amiss.

I was sure there was a hidden entrance somewhere, though for what purpose was beyond me. Roxon offered the theory, that the object was to frighten us out of the house by making us believe it was haunted. He was ever on the alert for the old woman, and regarded the intrusions with perplexed interest, rather than fear.

This opinion however, was not shared by Annabelle, and after several more glimpses of the old woman by Roxon and Mrs Greenwood, my wife made overtures of leaving. Somewhat surprisingly, the final blow was dealt by Tommy.

This time, it was Jamie who was asleep, and Tommy awake. An unknown woman in her early 20s, had appeared in the nursery. She had long black hair, which tumbled in curls over a loose fitting cloak. Like the man, she stood near the dying fire, peering sightlessly into its depths, and seemingly oblivious to the occupants of the room. She was very pale, and looked, in Tommy's words, both 'sorry and frightened'. There was, he said, 'something very peculiar about her eyes', and there was a dark streak across her throat.

The day before departure, the children were playing in the back garden, and I asked them to point out the spot where they'd seen the old woman searching. They were in complete accord as to the area, so I suggested that they might like to undertake one more treasure hunt, and encouraged them to dig.

To this day, I cannot explain why I did this, but in any event, the venture bore fruit – a skeleton wrapped in a decayed black cloak.

We never discovered their identities, nor the reason for the murder, but on one point Annabelle and I are both agreed. Our next sojourn, would involve a hotel.

3
THE ABDITORY

Dr David Gregory,
16 Oxbridge Lane,
Ealing,
London

15th April, 1883

My dearest Gregory,

As you will recall, when I took my departure from you on Wednesday last, I had every intention of staying with my cousin, Lord Emmet Durlish, for a month. You will therefore be shocked to learn, that I am returning to town forthwith, and that my bronchial condition, for which your prescription of 'respite and clean fresh air', was the reason for my sojourn, has been superseded by...terror. Indeed, upon my return, I would be exceedingly grateful for your immediate ministration, both as a friend and as a medical practitioner.

Brown, the dastardly fellow, has not divulged your final utterances to him whilst we stood at the railway station. However, if it were something along the lines of, 'take care of your master', then never has such cautionary advice been so profound, for had it not been for his diligence, I would be dead. I will try to set out events in reasonable order, but my mind is in such turmoil, and yes, possibly even disturbed, that logic and cohesiveness are proving rather elusive.

Thanks to the greed and lechery of Henry VIII, many monasteries were raped of their treasure and then destroyed. Yorkshire was no exception. The Dales are littered with remnants of his maniacal regime, as is Scarborough Park, the home of Lord Durlish. It is a beautiful rambling estate, with lush green fields, extensive woods and copses, and all the hunting and fishing a man could desire.

Having not seen Emmet for several years, and being a 'poorer relation', (only related by marriage), I was unsure of my welcome. However, Emmet was geniality itself, greeting Brown and myself with an effusiveness that I hardly deserved. It later occurred to me that, although Scarborough Park was a great estate, it is rather isolated, and therefore, devoid of that level of society within which a man of Emmet's standing would ordinarily mix.

Although my senior by ten years, I found his company most enjoyable. He obviously reciprocated my feelings, for later that evening, he showed me the letter you had written to him without my knowledge, explaining my condition and your remedy. Be not alarmed my friend. I will not chastise you, for I know you had my best interests at heart.

The following day after breakfast, we took a ride on two gentle mares. Emmet explained that he owned several powerful hunters and two strong racehorses, but thought it prudent that my first introduction to his estate, should be under conditions of sedateness. We rode past several of his tenements, all of which I was pleased to note, were in good order, and upon skirting the perimeter of a small wood, came to a clearing in which stood a large stone building. Although clearly very old, it was in remarkable condition.

"This," he explained, "is the Abbey of St. Frith."

"Who?"

"I've never heard of him either. It was probably one of those obscure religious orders that established itself in England to escape persecution somewhere else. During Henry VIII's vile reformation, all the surrounding buildings were destroyed, but this one, for some unknown reason, was left intact. Would you like to go in?" I was suddenly filled with a feeling of apprehension, as though some instinct, whilst not exactly ringing alarm bells, was warning me to proceed judiciously. Mistaking my hesitancy for something else, Emmet added, "I assure you, it's perfectly safe. There might be the odd spider or two, but there's nothing that can harm you."

Not wishing to appear cowardly, I nodded in ascent and we dismounted. "Do you not keep it locked?" I asked as he casually opened the heavy oak door, which creaked a little on its hinges.

"Not much point. The people around here are basically honest, and it is hardly accessible to passing travellers."

About 30 feet long by 20 feet wide, the interior was exactly as one might expect, musty and cobwebbed, with faded tapestries and an air of neglect. At the far end stood a long mahogany table, presumably the altar, and directly in front, were three rows of beautifully carved pews. With their rough and simple habits, it was not difficult to imagine how the monks would have polished the seats until they fairly shone, but which were now buried under a thick layer of dust.

I had expected it to be dark and dingy, but it was anything but, for dominating the west wall, was a magnificent stained-glass window. Now, I do not claim to be an expert on the subject, but even my untrained eye could see that there was something compelling in its simplicity.

"You noticed," said Emmet with a chuckle. "Curious isn't it? There is a legend of course, something to do with hidden treasure. There is an old book in the library called, The Lives of the Abbots', published in Cologne in 1712. While it doesn't name the Abbey, it describes the window exactly. The story goes, that as Henry's men were tearing down the buildings, a young monk concealed a vast quantity of gold somewhere in the monastery. Later, when Mary Tudor ascended the throne, he is supposed to have used the gold to pay for the window, designing it to his own specifications, as his coat of arms in the bottom right corner, attests. He also paid for a well in what was once the courtyard, adorning it with somewhat grotesque stone carvings. Most are eroded now, but one of them depicts a two-faced lion, possibly a reference to Henry's religious hypocrisy."

I studied the window more closely. There were three main panels, each containing a solitary monk. The first and third were holding a scroll, while the second was holding an open book. I could vaguely discern lines of writing on each, but the window was far too dusty to read them accurately. With very little additional detail, nor any apparent indication as to their identity, it was curious as to why three seemingly ordinary monks, had been given such a reverential honour.

"It's certainly enigmatical," I conceded, "but I don't quite understand where the legend comes in."

"Ah, yes, I forgot to mention that not all the gold was used, and that the residue is still allegedly hidden in the monastery."

"I presume you've looked?" I asked, but before he could answer, the Abbey door suddenly banged open, the unexpected clatter making us jump.

Brown and Emmet's man-servant, Vickers, stood in the doorway. I cannot vouch for Vickers, but I could tell from Brown's slightly wrinkled brow, that he was not best pleased.

"I apologise for startling you, my lord," said Vickers, but without any real contrition, "but Mrs Crompton is at her wits end. It is long past luncheon and…"

"Good gracious so it is," exclaimed Emmet, consulting his watch. He lowered his voice so only I could hear him, and although his words were derogatory, they were spoken with affection. "Mrs Crompton is my cook. She runs the kitchen with a tyrannical fist. The old battleaxe, I don't know what I'd do without her." Aloud he said, "We shall return immediately."

"How did you get here?" I said to Brown, still wondering why he was scowling. The answer became apparent the moment we stepped outside. A pony & trap was standing in the former courtyard, now virtually obscured by weeds and grass, and on which the pony was munching happily. Considering the distance travelled, and over some fairly rough terrain in parts too, I did not envy their return journey.

Later that evening, Emmet produced the old book from the library. He sat in an armchair and quietly smoked a pipe while I examined the contents. The velum cover and many of its pages were loose with age, so naturally I handled it with care. Along with the printed description, which was precise enough to verify its accuracy, on a separate piece of paper, someone had sketched the window. There were also three lines written in Latin, and beneath these, the translation.

First scroll, 'There is a place for gold where it is hidden'. The line on the book, 'They have on their raiment a writing which no man knoweth'. The second scroll, 'Seeker beware. The guardian is one with seven eyes'.

"Well?" said Emmet after about 15 minutes, handing me a glass of excellent brandy. "What do you make of it?"

I had only been in the 'clean fresh air' as you put it, for one day, and yet I was already feeling the benefit. My breathing was easier, and I had hardly coughed all day, that is to say, there was no sign of the previous hacking cough that left me sore and exhausted. I must also give credit to Mrs Compton for, 'battleaxe' or not, she was an excellent cook. I was therefore at ease for the first time in weeks and ready to discourse heartily.

"The use of tenses in the first scroll is significant. When you consider that the window was not erected until after the dissolution, if the three monks had indeed hidden a stash of gold from Henry's men, and remember, there is no evidence as to how many monks were involved, then the line should have read, 'There was a place for gold where it hath been hidden'."

Emmet slowly nodded his head. "'Was', instead of 'is'. Past tense instead of present. Nobody is going to pay a fortune for bad spelling."

"Which emphasises a second point. I don't think I have ever heard anyone use the word 'raiment' in relation to clothing. While it is a perfectly acceptable word, it is also extremely old-fashioned and rarely used nowadays."

"And the last line?"

"Ah, now there I am at a loss. You mentioned spiders just before we entered the Abbey, and I did consider the possibility of something resembling a spider, or spider-shaped, but compared to the cryptic nature of the other two lines, it seems a little too obvious."

We discussed the matter for several hours, and it

became increasingly apparent, that with the window as the only guide, the answer to the mystery, assuming there was one, lay within its confines. It was therefore with Emmet's blessing that the next morning, armed with supplies, cleaning rags, and decent horses, Brown and I went to the Abbey.

In all modesty, I don't think the window ever shone so brightly. Now that it was clean, and with the morning sun behind it, what little colour it contained, bounced off the flagstones like jewels. Mounted on a variegated red background, each monk was dressed in a long brown robe, with a broad black border around the hem. And yet for all its simple perfection, if the window did contain a secret, it was guarding it well. The only consolation, was that the extra light lifted the sombreness of the Abbey, so that the ghostly echo of chanting monks seemed to reach across the centuries.

I always said that Brown was a dastardly fellow, and due to his upbringing and training, it was he who uncovered the meaning of, They have on their raiment a writing which no man knoweth.

I had sent him outside to survey the exterior, while I sketched the window in finer detail. Upon his return, he coughed lightly and said, "Excuse me, sir, but why are your fingernails black?" He picked up several cleaning rags lying on the floor. "Look, these are streaked with the same peculiar dust."

Staring at the window, I willed my eyes to see what my brain would not…and they did see. The only 'black' of note, was the border around the hem of the habit. Moreover, it was the only section that was not translucent. Using a scrubbing brush and Brown's pocket-knife, I began to scrape the glass. Almost instantly, a patch of the brightest yellow appeared.

"It's some sort of paint or thick pigment," I announced excitedly, the flakes now falling even faster to the floor. "It must have been applied after the window was constructed." The blacking, having disintegrated with age, came off fairly easily, and in less than two hours, three inscriptions were revealed.

This discovery made it absolutely certain that the Abbey was keeping a secret. And what were the inscriptions? Oh, my dear Gregory, it was only the most hopeless jumble of letters ever conceived, 114 in total. I was, as you may imagine, utterly disconsolate. But then, as the saying goes, hope sprang eternal, and in a flash, I realised that it was a cipher. All I had to do, was find the key, and considering its age, it was likely to be of a simple nature.

I will spare you a laborious recital of the next 72 hours. Suffice to say that with Emmet's encouragement and use of his library, plus the translation from Latin to English as provided in the book, by the afternoon of the third day, I had broken the cipher. What happened next, you will no doubt attribute to recklessness, but in my defence, I own that this was the most exciting thing that had ever happened to me, and I defy any man to act rationally under such circumstances.

Emmet was not home, and though I longed to include him in the task at hand, impatience won the hour, so armed with tools, lamps, and a good length of rope, Brown and I set forth for the Abbey.

It was about six o'clock in the evening, and the beauty of the setting sun and the almost total silence, cooled my ardour, so much so, that the first feeling of foreboding made itself known. There was always the possibility that someone, ignorant of ciphers and guided by luck, might have stumbled on the treasure before me. Moreover, now that I had time to reflect, I was not entirely easy as to the meaning behind the guardian of the treasure.

Upon reaching the Abbey, and using nothing but our bare hands, Brown and I cleared the area around the well. As Emmet had said, most of the stone work had eroded away, but several reliefs were just discernable. I found the previously mention two-faced lion, and fragments of coats of arms. Somewhat curiously, the shield attributed to the young monk, as depicted in the bottom corner of the window, was relatively intact.

I stood back and examined the structure. It was square with an opening in one side. There was a protective arch over the well-head, to which was attached a horizontal beam to affix a rope. The question of depth was easily answered by the dropping of several pebbles. I judged it to be about 60 feet.

As to the interior, two lamps suspended on the rope, in every respect, provided illumination, for just below ground level and built into the masonry, were a series of stone blocks. Loosely speaking, a crude set of stairs.

It seemed too good to be true, and I wondered if the stones had been contrived to tip over when a weight was placed on them. Tying one end of the rope to the beam and the other end around my waist, I slowly began to descend. Brown was two steps behind me holding a lamp. I had elected to use a candle, for there was always the chance of an opening further down, and any draught would be registered quicker with a flickering flame than a lamp.

With extraordinary care, I felt every block before setting foot on it, and then scanned the wall for anything out of the ordinary. About two thirds of the way down, the blocks suddenly stopped. I could clearly see our lights reflected in the water below, and though the distance did not look great, I had no desire to jump in. Again, it was my dastardly fellow, Brown, who made the discovery.

"Sir," he whispered urgently, and pointed to an irregular area in the surface of the masonry. There was no mark, but the texture looked a little smoother than the rest. Moreover, when I touched it, my fingers came away black.

I withdrew a chisel from my pocket and lightly tapped the stone. There was an unmistakable hollow sound, and a lump of pitch fell off. In spite of what was to follow, even now, I cannot think of that moment without a sense of pride.

It took but a few more taps to expose a stone about 12 inches square, but as the last of the pitch fell away, my former anxiety in relation to 'the guardian', returned with force. Nevertheless, I was not about to retreat.

The mortar around the stone, as I discovered when I used the chisel to prize it loose, was just enough to keep it in place. Call it foolishness, but the moment the cavity was exposed, I hastily stood on the preceding block lest something should escape. I caught a whiff of stale foul air and waited for several minutes. Then, with candle in hand, which was trembling from my emotions rather than any draught, I inserted it into the cavity.

The hole went some way back, and I could see several dark-coloured objects towards the rear. There was nothing immediately in front of the hole. I put my arm in and gingerly reached for an object. My fingers touched something solid and leathery, and though heavy, it moved more easily than expected. Then, as I started to pull it forward, Brown let out a strangled cry and fled up the steps with the lamp. I had no time to contemplate his action, for at the same moment inside the cavity, 'something' grabbed hold of my wrist. The candle fell and I was plunged into darkness.

My dear Gregory, the next few moments stretched an eternity. I am now acquainted with the extremity of terror that a man can endure before insanity takes hold.

The creature, for there is no other word to describe it, scuttled up my arm and clung to my chest. Naturally I tried to fling it from me, and it was then that I saw it clearly, for as I touched it, it glowed and pulsated fiery red. Its shape was reminiscent of a crab, and was equal in size to a dinner plate. I was conscious of a face with many eyes, and as it pressed against my own its extraordinarily long legs, or arms or whatever they were, encircled my body.

According to Brown, I screamed like a beast and fell backwards onto the steps. I can only assume that the creature returned to the cavity. Brown did not see it, which undoubtedly was most fortunate, for if he had, he might not have had the presence of mind to haul me, now unconscious, up the steps. His explanation as to why he fled in the first place, only adds to the nightmare. Omitting his dramatic and colourful rejoinders, this is what he told me later.

"You were busy with the hole when something dropped into the water from above. I looked up and saw a head draped in a cowl, looking down at us. As I ran up the steps, the lamp shone on his face. It was old and sunken and covered in what I can only describe as cobwebs. He was also laughing fit to burst. When I finally reached the top, there was nobody in sight. I began to look around, making sure that he wasn't crouching behind the well. The next thing I knew, you were screaming something terrible, and when I looked over the edge, you were lying on your back on the steps."

There is not much more to tell. We made it back to Scarborough Park. Fortunately, Emmet was still out, so feigning a recurrence of my bronchial condition to explain my pallor to Vickers, Brown and I retired to my room, where after ministering to my needs, including conveying my clothes to his own room, he went to the kitchen for a bite of supper.

I spent a miserable night, the whole thing was ghastly and abnormal. However, of one thing I am absolutely sure. All through the darkened hours, someone, or something, was loitering outside my door. It wasn't just the faint noises, but a hideous smell of mould, much stronger than could have emanated from my clothes, which as I stated, Brown had already removed.

With the first glimmer of dawn, the smell and the noises faded away. This convinced me that the thing was primarily a creature of darkness, and that whosoever replaced the stone, for I was equally convinced that it must be done, would not be harmed. As I write this letter, Brown, under strict and explicit instructions, is effecting remedies to the stone and the window.

I shall not, of course, divulge more to Emmet than he already knows. I think you will agree, that it is imperative that the secret of St. Frith's Abbey, remain buried. I shall shortly take my leave, and as I said at the outset, return to town forthwith, where I hope to find you waiting at the station.

Yours affectionately,

Marswell Townsend.

4
MIRROR IMAGE

Although born a year apart, Emily and Gilly were so extraordinarily alike, that they were often mistaken for twins. Their father, Colonel Adamson, a proud, sensible man, was officer-in-charge of a regiment in India. When his wife died of cholera, duty and propriety dictated that the girls be sent to relatives in England, and to this end, Emily, the eldest, was placed in the care of Miss Adamson, the Colonel's sister, while Gilly was sent to Lady Lacy, her maternal aunt. The Colonel would have preferred that his daughters remain together, but neither lady was inclined to take on the responsibility of two girls. Moreover, if both had been placed with one lady, the other would have regarded it as a slight.

If the Colonel thought he had served his daughters well, he was only half right. Lady Lacy lived in a small but comfortable house in Devon. Kind and intellectual, her sweet disposition was counter balanced by a rarely compromised iron-will. She was well-respected in local society, and raised Gilly to be an educated and liberal-minded woman, with graceful manners and a wealth of culture. The two were very fond of each other.

Miss Adamson on the other hand, was rigid in ideas, narrow in sympathy, and harboured a plethora of prejudices. She was repressive to the point, that literary luminaries such as Shakespeare, Pope, Scott, and Byron, were taboo. No work of imagination was allowed in the house, except for apocalyptic literature, and even then, her opinion was often contradictory. No prison with contracting walls, could have squeezed more life out of Emily than her Aunt.

The sisters hardly ever met, and for Emily the closest to excitement was a missionary meeting. On a rare visit to London, Gilly and Lady Lacy, had called to ask if they might take Emily to the theatre. Miss Adamson had looked horrified, and had expressed her opinion of the stage and its patrons. She would not 'imperil Emily's soul' by allowing her to attend. It was only thanks to her iron-will, that Lady Lacy restrained her tongue.

After her Aunt's refusal, Emily had burst into tears and run to her room. Unable to control her rage, she had then grabbed a book of sermons and torn it to pieces. Her Aunt, as she was wont to do, had entered Emily's room without knocking, not to explain, but to chastise.

"Emily," said Miss Adamson when she saw the wanton destruction, "you are but a child consumed by wrath." Emily being 17 was of no consequence.

"Why may I not hear music, or experience the gaiety of life that other girls my age do?"

"Because those girls are nothing but harlots, and all gaiety is heinous!"

Emily, her eyes burning with hot angry tears, for the first time in her life challenged her Aunt's convictions. "If God hates all that is fine and beautiful, then why did he create the peacock or humming-bird, instead of flooding the world with grotesque bats and owls? And I will thank you not to call my sister a harlot."

"Wicked child, you have a carnal mind."

"Is that your best answer – to insult me?" Emily clutched at her chest. It was suddenly painful. "But you can't answer, can you? Why? Because your perverse piety doesn't have an answer. You have exposed yourself for the hypocrite you are. The worship of God is supposed to provide comfort, not instil fear." She could hardly breathe. "Once I am of age, I shall leave this place forever..." another pain shot through her chest, "...and indulge in everything happy in life that you have suppressed." She fell back onto the bed. "I...I...Get out!"

Miss Adamson's letter to her brother, informing him of the death of his daughter from a heart attack, evinced not the slightest sympathy. True to form, she dwelt on Emily's faults, expressing her opinion that, "...as the girl at the end, rather than piety and goodness, craved all things immoral," she doubted the redemption of her soul. During the funeral, to which only five people attended, she was invited to say a few words by the grave. However, her opinion, along with self-justified embroidering, was expounded to such an extent, that the vicar seemed on the verge of asking her to be quiet.

At the conclusion of the service, Lady Lacy guided a sobbing, red-eyed Gilly to her carriage, and then found pretext to be alone with the Aunt. "Miss Adamson," she began, speaking quietly so as not to be overheard, "I find your manner and lack of Christian charity, abominable. How my sister endured your deplorable sanctity when you visited your brother in India, is testament to true piety. I shall, once the year of mourning has passed, in Emily's name, expose her sister to every aspect of society at my disposal. I sincerely hope our paths will never cross again, but should that unfortunate day transpire, make no mistake, madam, you will be treated with the same cold-hearted indifference you have displayed today."

A year later, Lady Lacy rented a house in London for the season. Gilly was now of an age to be introduced to society, and her first function, was a ball at the home of Felicity Andover, the Countess of Belgrave, a great friend of Lady Lacy. On the afternoon of the ball however, the wise old lady began to wonder if she had not commenced Gilly's social education, too ambitiously.

"Gilly," she said with a touch of exasperation, "will you settle down? You've been like a cat on hot irons all day."

"Oh, Aunty, I'm nervous and excited at the same time. I want to enjoy myself, but I don't want to embarrass you by doing something foolish."

Lady Lacy smiled. "If Miss Adamson were here, she would chastise you most profoundly, and then lock you in your room."

Gilly shuddered. "Oh, don't remind me of that dreadful woman. Poor Emily, how she must have suffered." She paused then went on tentatively, "I heard what you said to Miss Adamson at the funeral."

"Really? Come here, child." Gilly sat on the footstool next to the chair, silent tears rolling down her face. Lady Lacy took her hands. "I meant every word I said to that vile woman, but you are wrong if you think that your introduction to society, is solely to fulfil the promise I made to honour Emily's memory. You have been as a daughter to me, and I know for absolute certainty, that your mother would have approved. Now, stop crying, otherwise you'll be going to the ball with puffy eyes. Go upstairs, wash your face, and have a rest. I'll make sure you're called in plenty of time."

There was a gentle tap on the door, and Marchbanks, a middle-aged woman in service to Lady Lacy for nigh on ten years, entered carrying a gold box tied with ribbon. "Excuse m'lady, but this just arrived for Miss Gillian."

With a flush of excitement highlighting her cheeks, Gilly opened the box. It was a blood-red camellia. "Oh," she cooed, "it's beautiful. I wonder who sent it."

"Read the card," said Lady Lacy with bemusement, "but don't handle the flower before you're ready, otherwise it will bruise."

Gilly carefully extracted the card. "Why, it's from Jeremy…I mean, Captain Andover."

"A fine young man," said Lady Lacy. "Marchbanks, Gilly is going to rest before getting dressed. Please take a cup of tea to her room."

"It's alright, Aunt. I feel much better now."

"That may be so, but your eyes are still puffy. Now, run along dear, I have some letters to write."

In her bedroom, Gilly placed the box on her dressing table. She touched a petal with the tip of a finger. How kind of Jeremy to think of her, but then, knowing his character as she did, she wouldn't have expected anything less.

She looked at her reflection in the mirror. Dimples notwithstanding, she was quite winsome when she smiled. Her lips still had something of the child-like rosebud about them, her face was pleasant and unlined, and her thick dark hair was healthy and glossy.

Marchbanks entered with the cup of tea. "You will look beautiful," she said, indicating the lacey white ball gown hanging on the wardrobe door. On the floor beneath the dress, were a pair of matching satin slippers.

Gilly exchanged her clothes for a wrap, and then lay on the bed. "I'm not the least sleepy you know."

"You heard what your Aunt said," said Marchbanks bossily. "You are to rest before dressing."

Gilly pointed to the dressing table. "Look what

Captain Andover sent me," she said with a yawn, suddenly unaccountably tired.

"Very pretty." Marchbanks went to draw the curtains, but Gilly stopped her.

"No, I want to look at the sky; it's such a lovely afternoon." She did not add, 'and somewhere up there, Emily is smiling down on me'.

Gilly fell into a dreamless sleep. It was still light outside when she opened her eyes. She jumped out of bed, ran to the dressing table, and frantically began brushing her hair. A moment later however, she stopped dead. The camellia lay in the box, but instead of pristine condition, it was damaged. There were signs of withering, and several petals had fallen off.

"Oh, you're finally up," said Marchbanks, entering the room carrying a tray.

"Never mind the tea, we'll have to hurry otherwise I'll be late for the ball, and I don't want to miss a moment."

"Aw, Miss, you will have your little joke. The ball was a success, and so were you. Lady Lacy almost cried when she saw you in your gown, but then, you already know that."

"I know nothing of the sort. Now please, hurry up and help me dress."

"But…Miss, you've already been to the ball." Walking over to the chair where it lay, Marchbanks held up the gown. The white satin was no longer smooth, and the train showed signs of being trodden on. She then pointed to the slippers, which also bore marks of wear.

Gilly was stunned. "I…I don't remember."

"I'm not surprised, Miss. When Captain Andover…"

"Captain Andover?" she interrupted, her voice somewhat shrill.

"Why, yes Miss. Captain Andover escorted you and her ladyship 'ome, and when he kissed your hand, you ran up the stairs giggling like a schoolgirl."

Gilly clutched her head, her breath coming in short rapid gasps. "Um…look, Marchbanks, would you mind leaving me alone. Tell my Aunt I'll be down shortly."

Gilly bathed her face in cold water. She could not remember anything about the ball. Hoping it would provide a clue, she picked up the programme and read it with dazed eyes. She recognised the initials, JA for Jeremy Andover, apparently they had danced several times together, but the other initials, like the ball itself, were unknown.

Twenty minutes later, Gilly went downstairs and entered the dining-room, where Lady Lacy was eating poached eggs. "My dear, you did not need to rise so early. After all, you practically danced the soles off your shoes."

Gilly's bewilderment deepened. She had to discover more. "And you? Did you enjoy yourself?"

"As much as an old lady can. I like to watch young people dancing. It reminds me of my former days. You might not think it to look at me now, but my programme was always full, as was yours, which is probably why you looked rather pale and tired by the end of the evening."

As soon as breakfast was finished, Gilly escaped to her room. She needed time to think. The only possible explanation was that she was a somnambulist. What had she said and done while unconscious? What if she'd awakened in the middle of a dance? Somehow, she must have dressed, gone to the ball, returned home, removed the gown and donned the wrap again, and all while asleep.

"By the way," said Lady Lacy the following day, "I

have secured tickets for Carmen, at Her Majesty's theatre. We shall be a small party, but I think you will enjoy it."

The news acted on Gilly's troubled mind like a balm. "Oh, how wonderful. Dear Aunty, how good you are. I know some of the music of course, the Toreador song, but I have never heard the entire opera. What should I wear? Is black too mournful?"

"I think your beaded black dress would be perfect, especially if you wore your mother's pearls as well." Lady Lacey paused then added mischievously, "I'm sure Captain Andover will approve."

"Aunty!" said Gilly in a mock scandalised voice, blushing to the roots of her hair.

Two evenings later Gilly went into the conservatory and sat in a wicker chair. It was not quite time to dress, and having obtained the libretto, she wanted to study the opera before departing. She began to hum Toreador, but the next thing she knew, not only was she stiff and sore, but the first glimmer of dawn was peeking through the windows. She ran into the hall and drawing-room, but they were dark, deserted, and cold. Even the fire in the kitchen showed little sign of life.

Confused and light headed, Gilly clung to the banister as she made her way to her room. She turned on the light. Her black dress lay across the bed as though it had just been removed. There were also gloves, a fan, and a slightly crumpled opera programme.

Gilly sank into a chair and began to cry. A short time later, Marchbanks entered with morning tea. "Did you have a pleasant evening, Miss?"

Gilly looked up. She did not need a mirror to know that her face was pale and blotchy. "Is my Aunt awake yet?"

"Yes, she's in the dining-room. Wonderful constitution her ladyship has. She never ceases to amaze me."

Gilly dressed quickly and went downstairs, her mind in turmoil. "Aunty," she went on after preliminaries were exchanged, "would you mind if I saw a doctor? I don't think I am quite well."

"Oh? What is the matter?"

Not wishing to frighten her Aunt, Gilly had already thought of a plausible explanation. "I seem always to be tired, yet when I try to sleep, I'm wide awake."

"Hmm…perhaps it has all been too much for you. I did think you were looking very pale again last night. Doctor Groves is the man to see. I shall send him a message asking him to call. Meanwhile, a good breakfast will not do you any harm."

Gilly smiled in appreciation but could only pick at her food, and when the medical man arrived, she received him alone in the drawing-room. She did not mince words. "Doctor Groves, I believe I am walking in my sleep. I have now had two experiences where I have gone out and apparently enjoyed myself, yet I can remember nothing."

"Has this ever happened before?"

"No. It started after I came to London for the season."

"And how were you roused? In other words, how did you become aware that you were sleep-walking?"

"I just woke up. One can hardly attend a ball and the opera without remembering it, and yet that is exactly what happened."

"Most extraordinary. Are you sure you went to the ball and the opera?"

Gilly began wringing her hands. Her voice held a note of hysteria as she answered, "That's the point. All the evidence suggests that I did, and yet I don't remember."

Doctor Groves patted her shoulder. "Calm yourself Miss Adamson..."

As he said her name, Gilly felt such a sudden and inexplicable wave of wrath, that it took a tremendous effort not to scream.

"Gilly? Gilly? Are you alright?"

"Oh...yes, sorry Doctor. What were you saying?"

"I was about to ask you if Lady Lacy had accompanied you on both occasions."

"Yes."

Doctor Groves thought for a while and then said, "I don't think this is a case of somnambulism, more like, lapse of memory. Have you ever suffered from that?"

"Not in the way you mean. We are all apt to forget things at times."

"I think," he said slowly, "that coming out has been too much for you. Some girls are naturally ebullient - some too much for their own good, but yours is a quieter disposition, and therefore, your nerves cannot stand the strain. Like anything that is stretched to the limit, sooner or later, it will snap."

"But what shall I say to my Aunt? She has gone to considerable expense to give me this season."

"Leave that to me. I will say that you have become a little over-wrought, and must be spared too much excitement. I think you'll find that now you've told someone about it, you'll start to feel better. But, please don't misinterpret this as the remedy. The body is capable of much more than we, as yet, understand. Just slow down, get plenty of rest, and if anything else happens, call me immediately."

"Thank you, Doctor Groves."

Over the following days, Gilly followed his advice to

the letter, as did Lady Lacy. She began by pruning their engagements to an acceptable minimum, and even in the small matter of writing a note of apology, Gilly was not allowed to raise the pen.

At the end of a week's respite, Gilly felt much better, but she was also restless and bored. Lady Lacey seemed to sense this, for she said over breakfast, "What do you say to seeing the new play at the Gaiety Theatre tonight? Felicity has a private box, and she has invited us to join her."

Gilly beamed with pleasure. "We do seem to have been rather quiet of late," she said, kissing the old lady's cheek.

The evening proceeded without a hitch. Captain Andover was his usual, charming, vastly agreeable self, talking to Gilly between the acts. During a lull in the performance, he leaned closer and said, "I have been deputised to ask you something."

Gilly felt a rush of excitement. "What is it?"

"We are attending the Henley Regatta on Sunday. Will you join us?"

"Oh Jer...um, Captain Andover." Gilly blushed. "I should love to," though in truth, she couldn't remember where Henley was.

Two days later, Lady Lacey stood in the drawing-room, and somewhat unusually, was looking at Gilly disapprovingly. "To judge by the weather, it will be rather chilly on the river today, and your muslin dress simply won't do."

Gilly thought for a moment then said, "My grey suit, a black cummerbund, and my white straw hat. How about that?"

"Perfect, but you've only got about twenty minutes to change. If we're not ready when Felicity arrives to collect us, Countess or not, she'll have the hide off us."

Gilly dashed upstairs and changed her clothes. Then, not wanting to show her ignorance, for she still couldn't remember where Henley was, she went to a room that was more library than parlour, and found a book of maps. She sat at a table and opened the book. England was spread across two pages. Then, as she began to trace the course of the Thames with a finger, without warning, her head fell forward onto the table.

Gilly slowly opened her eyes. Where there had been daylight before outside the window gaslights were shimmering in the encroaching darkness. Suddenly, the front door slammed and Marchbank's voice came floating up the stairs.

"Come inside and get warm. I have a pan of hot chocolate ready."

Gilly ran to the top of the stairs. Then, with a shock that turned her blood to ice, she saw herself coming up the stairs. Dressed in a grey suit and white straw hat, the apparition walked straight passed her and entered her room.

Gilly clung to the banister for dear life. She must get help, but she seemed to have lost the power of speech. Like a child taking its first tentative steps, she tottered down the stairs into the drawing-room. She stood in the doorway for a moment, staring sightlessly at Lady Lacy, and then collapsed.

When Gilly came to her senses, she was lying on the sofa. Marchbanks was applying a cold compress to her head, while Lady Lacy, her expression extremely alarmed, was holding a bottle of smelling-salts.

"Oh, Aunty, I saw…"

"Calm yourself, child. You should not have run

upstairs to change your clothes. Obviously you have not recovered as much as we thought. I have sent for Doctor Groves. He will know exactly what is to be done. Marchbanks, beef tea at once."

Doctor Groves duly arrived, but unlike the previous occasion, Lady Lacy did not withdraw. She did however, retreat to the window while he conducted the examination. "Your niece is completely spent," he pronounced. "The sooner you return to Devon, the better. In the interim, I will arrange for a tonic to be delivered. I also suggest that someone stay with her tonight."

"Marchbanks will do it. She is extremely fond of my niece, and will ensure no harm befalls her."

Had she not felt so weak, Gilly would have cried for joy. She was dreading returning to her room alone, but how could she convey the fact to the Doctor without alerting her Aunt? She managed, by squeezing his hand, to gain the Doctor's attention. She then looked at him pleadingly, telling him with her eyes, that there was more to it. He seemed to understand, for he gave her a barely perceptible nod of his head.

"I will call again in the morning," he said to the room at large. "Until then, she is to be confined to bed with nothing, I repeat, nothing, to excite her."

"Come along, Miss Gillian," said Marchbanks when he'd gone, "we'll soon have you right as rain." But upon reaching the bottom of the stairs, Gilly hesitated. Naturally, Marchbanks misinterpreted the gesture. "If you haven't the strength to climb, just lean on me. Don't you worry your pretty little head, Miss Gillian. Nothing will happen to you when old Marchie is around."

Gilly gathered her courage as she entered her bedroom. The straw hat and grey dress, were flung across a chair as though she had just taken them off. Lying in bed, her mind was a whirl of disjointed thoughts. What was the significance of the apparition? What was the connection, if any, to the bouts of sleep-walking? After a glass of hot milk and a dose of the prescribed tonic, and with Marchbanks ensconced in an armchair not eight feet away, Gilly finally fell asleep.

When Doctor Groves arrived the next morning Gilly made a point of speaking to him alone, explaining in the minutest detail, what had occurred on the stairs. "It was horrible," she concluded, "far worse than before. I saw myself as clearly as I see you. I can only conclude that your earlier diagnosis, that I am a somnambulist, is correct."

"Actually, Miss Adamson…" Once again at the mention of her name, Gilly felt a strange, unaccountable wrath. She fought against it as the Doctor continued, "…that was your diagnosis, not mine. However, you are closer to the truth than you realise. I gave the matter considerable thought last night, and this is what I think happened. You did go to the regatta, but whilst descending the stairs after changing your clothes, you woke up, but your conscious mind was still focused on events in the intervening period."

"In other words, two real memories amalgamated."

"Precisely. After changing your clothes, in the moment between waking and sleeping, you recalled yourself in your regatta costume coming up the stairs. This fragment of memory manifested itself as a vision. In reality, you saw nothing. This is not as uncommon as you might think. Take a person suffering from the DT's for example. The patient is convinced that he sees rats gnawing at his feet, or strange creatures climbing the walls. But he does not.

They are delusions formed in the brain as a result of the malady."

"So, I really attended the ball and the opera and the boat-race?"

"I have no doubt of it." Doctor Groves unexpectedly chuckled. "The propinquities and foibles of a first London society are enough to send anyone quite mad."

Gilly smiled in spite of the predicament. "That is the best thing I've heard in weeks. But, will these memory lapses happen again?"

"I don't know. In a manner of speaking, it's up to you. It is your brain that created the problem. Ergo, only your brain can solve it. However, as the trouble started after you arrived in London, I have already suggested to Lady Lacey, that you return to Devon sooner rather than later." He smiled and stood up to take his leave. "You know, in a way, you are most fortunate."

"How so?"

"Because you are escaping a system that, by its very nature, is riddled with scandal and disgrace. Believe me, many young ladies have discovered to their cost, that mixing with the well-to-do does not consist of airs & graces and expensive ball gowns. At the door, he paused and said, "You are cut from a very different cloth. London is not for you. Your happiness lies elsewhere. Go home, get married, and raise a family." He lowered his voice and added mischievously, "I'll even tend the birth." Gilly burst out laughing. The Doctor's jovial bed-side manner was certainly unique and pleasant.

Later that day, Captain Andover called at the house, and was dismayed to hear that Gilly was unwell. "I thought she looked ill at the boat-race," he said to Lady Lacy. Though he did not see Gilly, he spoke to Lady Lacy for almost an hour, and when he eventually departed, he had a satisfied smile on his face.

The following morning when he returned, Gilly had recovered enough to be sitting in the drawing-room. The Captain expressed his delight at seeing her up and about again. Lady Lacy rose from her chair, muttered something about seeing to luncheon, and left them alone. The moment the door was closed, Captain Andover rushed over and took Gilly's hand.

"My darling, how can I ever thank you? I know it was a hurried affair, but time was against us, what with you returning to Devon, and my expected recall to my battalion. But, as the thing was done with such haste, I came here to repeat my offer of marriage. No doubt you have since reflected on my proposal. Dearest Gilly, please tell me you have not changed your mind."

Shrinking back a little, Gilly lowered her eyes and looked absently at the floor. "There is something I have to tell you, and it may be you who changes your mind."

"It would need to be something very serious in order to make me do that."

"It is. I am suffering from lapses of memory. I don't even remember the ball or..." He sealed her lips with a kiss. Gilly did think of resisting, but only for a moment. Perhaps this was, literally, just what the Doctor ordered.

"Yes," she said when they broke apart, "yes, I will marry you."

"As I explained to you at the boat-race, our engagement cannot be long. I will be ordered to Egypt soon, and I have every intention of taking my wife with me."

Gilly clung to his strong broad shoulders, tears of happiness running down her face. It then occurred to her, that there was an obstacle. "But what about my father's consent?"

"I shall wire him my full particulars. I have no doubt that with a corroborating wire from Lady Lacy, who approves of our marriage by the way, your father will give his consent."

Gilly gasped. "Oh my goodness, what about Aunty? She will be awfully lonely without me."

"No she won't. That aspect is already settled. In time, she will rent out the house in Devon and join us in Egypt. We will bury the dear old girl up to her neck in sand and make a second Sphinx out of her. If nothing else, it will bake the rheumatism out of her bones, but perhaps we shouldn't tell her that."

The next few weeks were a whirlwind of activity, though much to Gilly's annoyance, she was often ordered to rest. Still, there were some appointments where her presence was compulsory, such as when Mrs Thomas, the dressmaker, and Miss Crock, the milliner, were consulted as to her trousseau. Patterns and fabrics suitable for a hot climate, had to be selected, made, and fitted.

Lady Lacy was a great supporter of local industry, and with organisational skills to rival the Duke of Wellington, she soon set businesses in motion. The little post office was kept extraordinarily busy, for in addition to their usual services, as the invitations went out, so the wedding presents rolled in. Gilly wrote every letter of acknowledgment and thanks herself, along with a note to Captain Andover every day, meant for his eyes only.

The great day dawned bright and sunny, and gradually, the six bridesmaids, garnered from some of Lady Lacy's most intimate, and as she put it, eminently sensible' friends, arrived at the house. Dressed in pretty yellow gowns with a headpiece of primroses, each wore a gold and topaz brooch, previously presented by Captain Andover as an expression of thanks.

The page-boys were in green velvet, with white knee-breeches and ruffled lace, while the dining-room had been given over to the display of the gifts. Even the horse & carriage and driver, which was to convey the happy couple to the railway station, were decorated with bunting.

With the exception of a small travelling trunk, the remainder of Gilly's trousseau and belongings, were already on their way to Egypt. She stood in the drawing-room touching a pewter salt & pepper pot, a gift from the children at the Sunday school. She sighed as Lady Lacy entered the room.

"What am I going to do with four salt & pepper sets?"

"Once you're settled in Egypt and know what other items you require, I can exchange them in lieu before I come out."

"Not these," said Gilly affectionately, fingering the pewter pots again.

"Well, if I've overlooked anything, I hope it is minor."

Gilly's voice was choked as she said, "Dear Aunty, how good you have been to me. If only...if only Emily were here. I think of her all the time. I know this will sound silly, but sometimes, I'm sure I feel her presence."

"And I am equally sure she will be with you today." Aunt and niece embraced, tears of sorrow mingling with those of pride.

Marchbanks entered the room. "Excuse me, Miss Gillian, but two more wedding presents have just arrived."

"I'll attend to them," said Lady Lacy. "You, my dear,

had better go and get dressed, otherwise you'll be late for your own wedding."

"Would you like me to help?" said Marchbanks eagerly.

"No," said Gilly slowly. "At least, not yet. I'd like to be alone for a few minutes." She cast a glance at Lady Lacy, who smiled in understanding.

Gilly sat at her dressing-table and stared at her reflection in the mirror. In less than an hour, she would be Mrs Jeremy Andover. She found a scrap of paper and a pen, but as she leaned forward to practise writing her new name, a stab of pain shot across her back. She reached around and rubbed it. The preparations for the wedding, whilst undertaken with happy gusto, had nevertheless been exhausting. In addition, she had not gone to bed until two o'clock, and was up again at eight. If she didn't want to hobble down the aisle, she would have to lie down for a while.

When Gilly opened her eyes, the first sound she heard was the ringing of church bells. Then, turning her head, she saw herself sitting by the bed in full bridal regalia. Terror held her fast. She could not cry out. She could not move. All she could do was stare. Slowly, as though not to induce further fright, the apparition lifted the veil. It was Emily.

"Please don't be frightened. I will not hurt you. I love you too much for that. You hear the church bells? They are tolling for your wedding. I took your place and signed the register, but I am not Mrs Jeremy Andover, you are." She removed the gold wedding band from her finger and held it out.

"I don't understand," said Gilly, taking the ring and slipping it onto her finger.

"I died a miserable wretch. All I ever wanted was to be good and happy. Oh, Gilly, you have no idea how much I suffered at the hands of Aunt Adamson. But, my time is limited, and I will not dwell on her."

"But how did you get here?"

"When my spirit left my body, it lingered in a place that had neither substance nor form. I mean, I could feel something solid under my feet, and was surrounded by a swirling white mist, yet I was in a vast expanse of nothingness. Then, after a while, or so it seemed, for I had no conception of time, a very old man with a long white beard and carrying a staff, emerged from the mist. He said that, although he could not restore my life, he would grant me a month's grace before moving on, to enjoy the pleasures so cruelly denied me. Gilly, it was I who went to the ball instead of you. It was I who sat and watched Carmen. It was I who went to the regatta and accepted Captain Andover's proposal. In the case of the latter, you were already developing an affection for him, so I didn't think you'd mind. Can you ever forgive me?"

"Oh, Emily, of course I can."

"Here, you'd better have this back as well." As Emily stood up, the wedding dress fell to the ground, revealing a simple white shift. She raised her eyes to the ceiling, and spoke as though answering a question. "Yes, I am ready, I am satisfied."

"Wait!" Gilly knew she had but seconds before Emily disappeared. There was only time for one question. "If you could go and do anything you liked, why didn't you seek revenge on Aunt Anderson?"

Emily smiled, a beautiful, Madonna-like smile. "Because I know where she's going after she dies, and it's not where she thinks it is."

5
THE FLIP SIDE

She was a beauty, a magnificent example of 19th century technology, sleek and black, the chrome work shining like silver. I could tell by the grin on Albert's face that, like me, he was very proud of her.

"Are you sure you can handle her, Albert?"

"Oh, yes sir," he said with supreme confidence. "Mr Taunton down at the garage, he gave me lessons last weekend. When I collected her last night, I brought her the long way home to gain more experience. She's a little different to what you're accustomed to though. If you'll look sir, the gears are now on the left of the wheel instead of the right."

I checked my watch, and felt a pang of irritation. "I'd love to take her for a spin myself, but I'm due in London at midday. Alright Albert, take me to the railway station and show me what you can do."

I sat in the back and breathed deeply, taking in the smell of the pristine leather. Albert drove sedately down the driveway, the gravel crunching under the barely marked tyres. As he turned right I asked, "What's her top speed?"

"According to the meter, sir, sixty miles per hour, but I haven't had her passed thirty."

"So put your foot down," I goaded merrily. "Go on, be daring."

"Not with Tatterley Hill in front of us."

I peered through the windscreen at the approaching

monstrosity. Being less than half a mile from my gate, Tatterley Hill was the bane of my life, and to the unwary, deceptively dangerous. On the side we were approaching, there were three bends, the second rather sharp, while the other side was a long sweeping descent.

I leaned forward and rested my arms on the back of the driver's seat. "I will never understand when the authorities build a new road, why they just don't flatten out the bumps."

Albert chuckled. "Yes sir."

I was extremely fond of Albert. He was at least 35 years my senior, and was one of those rare breed of servants whose loss would be devastating should he ever leave. Not that that was ever likely for he'd been with the family for years.

I watched him manipulate the gears, and by the time we reached the station, I had a fairly good idea of the process.

"I'll be on the nine o'clock down train," I said, running a hand over the barely warm bonnet, and resisting the urge to kiss the car 'goodbye'.

I cannot recall what had taken me to London, for the intervening hours are a blur, yet from the time I returned to my country station, everything is extraordinarily clear. I exited the station and there she was, parked by the kerb with headlights as bright as two full moons, the 'woman' who had stolen my heart.

"I'll drive," I said to Albert, who had opened the rear door. "You can sit in the back for a change."

"Sir," he said as I climbed behind the wheel, "the gears are not the same. Perhaps I should drive."

It was foolish to learn a new system in the dark, but like all men with a new exciting toy, I was eager to try it. I bundled Albert into the back and then we set off.

It was five miles to my home, and everything was going smoothly until we began to ascend Tatterley. I put my foot down, determined to treat with scorn, the long but steep gradient. We had just cleared the brow when the trouble began.

I reached out a hand to change down gear, but the lever would not move. I didn't mind so much when the foot-brake failed to respond, but when I yanked the hand-brake and the car still didn't stop, that's when I became worried.

By this time, we were tearing down the hill. The lights were brilliant, and I managed to clear the first bend with relative ease. However, the second bend was fast approaching, and I had but seconds to think. Albert behaved splendidly. I should like that to be known. He was perfectly cool and fully alert, and seemed to read my mind.

"I wouldn't do it, sir. At this speed, if you clip the bank too high, she'll flip over. Turn the engine off and swing her gently from side-to-side, but make sure you're not hugging the bend as we turn."

Perhaps it was his instruction, perhaps it was sheer good luck, but in either event, we made it. We were still travelling at speed, and although the third bend loomed ahead, the gradient was much shallower.

The headlights caught the stone pillars that marked the entrance to my driveway. Once we hit the gravel, I could swing and spin the car, thereby inhibiting the momentum. I looked at the distance and the pillars, and had a mental image of a billiard ball being hit with force into a pocket. The analogy, though borne from panic, was apt. I judged the timing, took a deep breath, and swung the wheel.

Someone was shaking me awake, gently at first, and then a little rougher. I thought it was Albert, but when I opened my eyes and my vision cleared, I was astonished to see that it was Stanley Morton, an old college chum. With my senses still scrambled, I was prepared to take anything and everything at face value.

I was lying on the grass about 20 feet inside the driveway. People were moving about with candles and lanterns, and I could see that several bricks had been knocked out of the right-side pillar, and that the entire front of the car was smashed to pieces.

"Good lord, what a mess." I was about to make some other superfluous comment, when I heard a cry of pain.

Someone shouted, "The weight is on him. Lift it easy," and to my enormous relief I heard Albert say, "It's just my leg. Where's the master?"

"Here I am!" I shouted at the top of my voice, but as the people were preoccupied with dismantling the car, they did not appear to hear me.

Stanley laid a hand on my shoulder. His touch was curiously soothing. "Are you hurt? Any pain?"

I sat up, flexed my limbs, and tentatively touched my head. I was perfectly intact, and could not keep the surprise out of my voice. "None whatsoever."

"No, there usually isn't."

And then it hit me. "Stanley," I cried, "you're dead."

"That's all right old chap," he said with a grin, "so are you."

6
FAITHFUL TO THE CAUSE

Maxwell Thomas could not have been happier. A rural lad from deepest Devonshire, his sole ambition was to become a professional journalist, and after what he considered 'wasted' years writing overly sensational articles for penny papers, his application to join a popular London newspaper, was accepted.

Max arrived at King's Cross station one dull October morning, and after depositing his belongings in the 'left luggage office', sought his new boss. "I possess an observant mind and a ready pen," he said assuringly to the editor, a squat, round faced man with a perpetual sniff. "I can do good work for the paper."

"Guess we'll have to see about that," said the editor sceptically. "Have you lodgings?"

"No sir."

The editor sighed. "Try the back streets, they're usually cheaper," he said, pointing over his shoulder towards the back of the building. "Report to me at two o'clock tomorrow afternoon. You can start on the graveyard shift."

Undeterred, Max set off to find a new home. Unfortunately, the few pounds his parents had given him upon his departure, and his future small income, meant that a respectable hotel was out of the question. Nevertheless, his optimism was still high as he began to pound the pavements. The reality however, hit home, and he was astonished and appalled at the squalor in which some people, presumably induced by circumstance, were forced to live.

The best that could be said for the three storey, grime smeared boarding house at 34 Baxter Street, was that the windows and front door were clean. The landlady, Mrs Dixon, looked as old as the house. Her nose was large, her green eyes were small, and her face was a network of wrinkles.

The preliminaries having been settled, as Max followed her to the top of the house, he noticed that there was only one mounted gaslight on each landing, and judging from the lack of scorching on the wall, the flame was always kept low. The room was plain in every respect, with basic furniture and thread-bare carpet. Still, it was within his price range, and there was very little noise in the street outside.

"Here it is," she said in her snappy, high-pitched cockney accent. "It's the only room I have left, take it or leave it."

"Is there anyone else on this floor?" he asked, taking in a thin partition. It was so crudely made, that he could see the outline of the boards under the wallpaper. Clearly at some stage in its history the room had been much larger.

Mrs Dixon eyed him warily. "What do you want to know for?"

Max shrugged. "No particular reason. It's just nice to know who my neighbours are."

"There's no one except the gentleman next door." She jerked a thumb towards the partition. "But he keeps very much to himself. I doubt you'll ever see him."

"I see," said Max. "So, I'm more or less alone up here."

"Pretty much," said Mrs Dixon, her eyes glistening greedily as Max produced his purse. For better or worse, this was his new home.

As ordered, Max arrived for work the next day, and for the following two nights, did not return home until after 1 am. At first, Mrs Dixon had complained about being, "Awakened from me bed," but by the fourth night, and long after the nearby church clock had struck three, she reluctantly gave him a key.

The room proved comfortable enough, though his unusual hours prevented him from meeting other residents, including the gentleman next door. Except for his inclination to move about in the early hours, which he took little care to do quietly, Max had no conception of the man.

About the middle of the second week, Max returned home after a long day's work. It was two o'clock in the morning, and the gaslights on the landings were turned low as usual. Being excessively tired, his footing was clumsy in the virtual darkness. Yet nobody seemed disturbed by his undue noise, and the house remained still and quiet.

Peeling off his clothes, he was about to get into bed and read a book, when he suddenly stopped and listened. Someone was coming up the stairs. The heavy tread denoted a man, and the confident footfall announced that he was no stranger to the house.

Deciding that it could only be the gentleman next door, he was about to turn out the light when he was startled by a knock on the door. Was he finally to meet his elusive neighbour?

Max had scarcely taken a step across the room, when he heard the sound of the other door being opened and a man saying peevishly, "Father, you have the wrong room as usual. Come in here."

The door was slammed shut, quickly followed by more heavy footsteps and the sound of scraping chairs. The men seemed completely indifferent to their neighbour's comfort, for they made enough noise to wake the dead and, as they began to talk, Max jumped into bed and buried his head under the pillow. He did not want to listen, but in the quietude and darkness, snatches of conversation reached his ears.

"What do you mean you can't get it?"

"I might be able to get part of it, but…"

Max heard the sound of a dull thud, as though a fist had been banged on a table. "A part of it!" cried the elder man. "Oscar, we are facing ruin and disgrace. Part of it is next to useless. We need all of it, and only by marrying the girl can you get it. You know she is silly enough to give you anything, and so long as you give her a plausible excuse, she will not suspect. I give you my word that all will be repaid." There was a long pause, and Max guessed that the younger man was thinking. When the older man resumed, his voice was calmer but no less insistent. "Oscar, you must get it. Would you see me arrested for embezzlement when it could be avoided? Is our name to be cursed and spat upon?"

Max realised that he had been listening intensely. Moreover, it was likely that other people in the house had also overheard. Decency dictated that somehow, he convey the fact to the men. He began to cough loudly and persistently, but the voices continued as before, the son protesting and the father growing angrier. Max then groped in the dark for his book, and hoping it would not penetrate the cheap materials, tossed it lightly towards the partition. The voices went on unconcernedly. His attempts to alert the men had fallen on deaf ears.

Max climbed out of bed, turned up the light, and checked his watch. It was nearly 3 am. More concerned with sleep than the morality of his neighbours, he went into the passageway and knocked on their door. The conversation instantly ceased, and Max expected one of the men to appear and apologise, but the door remained closed. He knocked again, but as he did so, he became aware of a curious sensation. Although there was no light shining under the door, he was absolutely sure that someone was behind it. In addition, the house had taken on an aura of expectancy, as though it was waiting for something to happen.

Max shivered, but whether it was from the cold or the creepiness he could not have said. He put his mouth next to the keyhole. "Gentlemen, please do not talk so loudly. It is very late and I wish to sleep."

He listened but there was no answer. The stillness of the house began to press on him. He looked behind and down the stairs, hoping and yet fearing that something would break the silence.

Returning to his room, he paused to peer over the banister. The space below was a void of deep shadows, where anything or anyone could be concealed. Was it his imagination, or was there something swaying on the very bottom step? Was someone whispering and shuffling near the front door, the faint sound more inarticulate than the usual noises of the night?

"Don't be silly," he murmured, and went to bed, leaving the house and its inmates to themselves, while he slipped into dreams of home.

Peace reigned for the next two nights, but on the third night, when his consciousness was hovering between sleeping and waking, he was disturbed by a sound from the depths of the house. The window suddenly rattled. Max turned his head so sharply that he 'cricked' his neck. Moonlight spread across the floor, highlighting the carpet's shabbiness, but there was nobody forcing an entry. It was the wind, a howling portentous bluster.

Max settled down to sleep again, but a moment later he sat bolt upright. There *was* another sound, growing more distinct every second, and what's more, he'd heard it before.

"The old man," he whispered. He checked his watch by moonlight. It was half past two, roughly the same time as three nights earlier. Perhaps it was the slow rhythmic footfall, but he was suddenly assailed by a feeling of menace, as though the man was coming to get him.

Max stared at the door. Did the handle just move? His skin crawled and his hair seemed to stand on end. He was trembling all over when he heard something brush past the wall, followed by a loud knock on the adjacent door.

"Oh, so it's you." Max recognised the voice as Oscar's.

"Did you get it?" his father demanded, noisily closing the door.

Max, now slightly light headed with relief, was desirous of stopping the loud conversation, but curiosity and a sense of righteousness got the better of him. He had almost been frightened to death, and he didn't think it impertinent to discover the reason why.

"No, I didn't," said Oscar feebly. "I'm sorry father but I just can't do it."

There was a nauseating 'smack' and then a crash. Max threw back the blankets, ready to jump out of bed, certain that the father had just hit the son.

"You are weak!" the father angrily screeched. "How you came from my loins I will never know. Why, even your air-head fiancée has more gumption than you."

Oscar's voice was more steady as he countered, "Don't you dare speak of Gillian like that. I will not have her dragged into this unholy mess. Your troubles are of your own making, Father. I will not allow you to rob the innocent again, even at the cost of my honour."

His father's laugh was mocking and cruel. "Honour? Shall I show you the price of your honour?"

There were 10 seconds of dead silence and then…"Father!" A chair toppled over. "You…you…they're Gillian's jewels. You stole them."

"Of course I did. I knew you were too much of a coward to ask her, so I paid her a visit yesterday. This jewel case was just lying on a table." He dropped his voice to a malicious growl. "If she was stupid enough to leave them lying about, then she can hardly complain if they're stolen."

There were the sounds of a scuffle, the father hurling vile oaths as though they were weapons, his son with short, strenuous gasps. The fight did not last long, and Oscar evidently won, for a moment later he exclaimed, "You scoundrel, you will never have her jewels."

Suddenly, frighteningly, the house fell eerily quiet. Max's blood felt frozen in his veins, and as the seconds ticked past without any more sounds, his instinct screamed that something terrible had happened in the neighbouring room. He jumped out of bed, turned up the light, donned his shoes and a dressing-gown, and darted for the door. Then, as he was about to turn the handle, something caught his eye. A lower portion of the flimsy partition was bulging into his room. Moreover, the wallpaper was splitting under the strain of the bending boards.

Max stared in horrified fascination, for beneath the bulge, which was clearly the size and shape of a man's back, something dark and serpentine was creeping over the carpet. Stretching out a hand to touch it, at the moment of contact he snatched it away. His fingers were covered in blood.

He ran to the room and pounded on the door. "Open up! Open up I say!" There was no response. He tried the door. It was locked. One tremendous kick later and he fell headlong into the room.

Max sprang to his feet. Apart from the moonlight pouring through the uncurtained window, there was no sound, no movement, not even the semblance of a presence. The room was completely empty, horribly and miserably empty.

A light flashed into the room. Max spun around, his arm raised as though to fend off a blow, but it was only Mrs Dixon. Even so, Max took a step backwards. In the dim light cast by the candle in her hand, her expression was one of hideous triumph.

"Fancy a bit of prowling did ya?"

"My dear woman, something awful has happened in this room."

"No it didn't. I can never keep anyone on this floor longer than a month, though those who are sensitive catch on sooner. Nothing really happens, it's all sort of in your head."

"Look here," he said, holding out his bloodied hand, "did I imagine this?"

"Imagine what?"

Max looked at his hand. It was clean and white as usual. "I don't understand. It was covered in blood."

"Not to worry dearie, it's all over now." Mrs Dixon

spoke as if she was soothing a child after a tooth extraction. "Nothing else will happen now. I'm going back to bed."

"Oh no you're not," said Max, blocking her path to the stairs. "I want the truth."

Mrs Dixon pulled her shawl more tightly around her shoulders. "Not here. Come into my parlour and I'll explain, but mind you get dressed first. I have my reputation to think of."

Still bewildered, Max returned to his room. On his way downstairs however, he turned up the gaslights on the landings. After what he'd just experienced, nothing could induce him to place his safety in the hands of a penny-pinching hag.

"It's a performance," said Mrs Dixon, her scrawny hands hugging a steaming cup. To Max's surprise, she had made a pot of tea. "Once it's played out the spirits go away, that is, until the next tenant arrives. I told you there was a gentleman next door to make you feel easier in case you heard anything. You were all alone on the floor."

"Mrs Dixon, that was deceitful, perhaps even fraud."

"And who's going to prove it? The man who last had that room, was found dead in bed. Terribly pale he was, eyes bulging out of his head."

"Good God. How many times has it happened?"

Mrs Dixon put down her cup and began to count on her fingers. "Four times that I know of."

"And they all died in the room next to mine?"

"Yes, which is why I don't rent it out anymore." She lowered her voice and spoke in a confidential manner. "The house was getting a bit of a reputation, and being a poor widow, I had to curtail it, even though I can hardly carry the cost."

Max stared at her in disbelief. He did not know which shocked him the more, the number of deaths, or her callous indifference. "Who are the spirits?" he managed to ask.

"25 years ago, this house was a private residence, owned by a family named Steinbeck. I think they were German. Wilfred Steinbeck, the father, was some big-wig in the city. Well up in society they were. Anyway, one day, his only son Oscar, was found dead in his room."

"I presume you mean the two rooms minus the partition."

"Just so. The son was declared to have committed suicide after robbing his fiancée of her jewels. Mr Steinbeck buried his son and returned to Germany. However, many doubted the verdict."

"Why?"

"Because of the position of the stab wounds. I have never seen the performance myself, though I've heard them moving about often enough."

"So," said Max slowly, an idea forming at the back of his mind, "you've never heard the conversation between the spirits?"

Mrs Dixon shuddered. "Not bloomin' likely. Gives me the willies just thinking about it."

Max returned to his room. His stomach fluttered as he past the broken door, but journalistic instinct was fast conquering fear. He lay awake for some time, half listening for any sound next door, and half deep in thought. He had names, he had an approximate date, and he had a good grasp of the circumstances. Though not vindictive, a delicious smile spread across his face as he thought of Mrs Dixon. She did not have a clue, and if his guess was right, both she and the house were about to become famous, but for all the wrong reasons. He managed to snatch a few hours' sleep and then went to the office.

"Why, Mr Thomas," said the concierge in surprise, "you're early."

Max did not resent the fact that he was still restricted to the graveyard shift. On the contrary, he enjoyed it. "Things to do," he said evasively, and hurried to a vast underground vault, where a veritable sea of bookcases and shelves stored decades of newspapers.

"The Steinbeck case?" said the archivist, a tall spare man whose gaunt pallor reflected the fact that he rarely saw the sun. He checked his records and then pointed to an aisle. "Down there, third shelf from the top."

Max found the folios. They were covered in dust and had obviously not been opened in years. An hour later, he ran to the editor's office and rapped smartly on the door. "Boss," he panted excitedly, all sense of propriety temporarily forgotten, "have I got a story for you."

Many years later when Max published his memoirs, he declared that, although he had reported many famous and notorious events, his greatest moment of triumph, was when, after much persuasion, Scotland Yard raised the floorboards at 34 Baxter Street.

"It was a most singular honour," he wrote. "Discretion dictates that I not disclose her proper name, but Miss Gillian was still alive, and it was with tears in my eyes that I returned her jewels. She declared that she had always known Oscar to be innocent of the theft, but never imagined the depths to which his father had sunk."

Wilfred Steinbeck was never charged. He only survived his son by several years, and died in wretched circumstances. Mrs Dixon dined on her notoriety for some time. Everyone was keen to spend a night in the 'haunted room', and although many declared with much embellishment, that they'd heard a conversation, the alleged dialogue never came close to Max's experience. He always smiled when he heard of a so-called encounter, for in his heart, he was sure that the spirit of poor Oscar Steinbeck, was at rest, not that Mrs Dixon, would ever have admitted it.

7
THE GREY LADY

I am an old lady now, and although I may be enfeebled, there is nothing wrong with my mind or my wits, except on those days when rheumatism intervenes. They say that with wisdom comes age, but that's just hooey. What it really means, is that you've gathered a lot of facts and information that is of no use to anyone.

I do have one story you might be interested in though. It started in the winter of 1854. My family, which consisted of my mother, my sisters, my brother, and myself, were living in a rented house in a quiet village on the south coast of Ireland. I had not been well for some time, and my dear mother decided that an extended absence from the smog and foul air of my home town, would be of benefit. I admit that I was highly-strung, but it was not of a kind to render me morbid or fanciful.

I had no preconceived ideas about the house, nor any of its former occupants. It was somewhat old-fashioned, with moderately sized furnished rooms. Although we had free reign, there was one room we particularly ignored, not because of anything sinister, but because it was packed with old musty furniture, which to adventuresome and high-spirited girls, was not the least attractive.

Although this room was kept locked, the key resided in the door. I think I only ever stepped inside it twice. There were two or three old cabinets, a gloomy four-poster bed complete with moth-eaten curtains, rickety chairs and spider-legged tables, and in a corner, a spinet.

We had rented the house from a Captain Larchmont, though whether naval or military I could not say, for we never saw him, and all negotiations were conducted through an agent.

Captain Larchmont and his family, usually lived in the house all year round, but this particular year, they had decided to spend the winter on the Continent. It never occurred to us to doubt his ownership, and it was not until long after we had vacated the premises, that we learned that he was only a tenant, though a tenant of long standing.

The people of the village were mostly fisherfolk, though we never became particularly acquainted with any of them, while the doctor and the clergyman, Mr Conroy, were relative newcomers. The latter took to dining with us, as my brother had been introduced to him whilst scouting for a suitable location.

The first few weeks were glorious, peace and quiet and plenty of fresh air. Then, in March 1855, I was getting dressed for dinner when my sister Helen entered my room.

"Do hurry up. Are you making yourself extra smart for Mr Conroy?"

Although it pained me to cast aspersions on a man of the cloth, I did not like him, for not only did he 'talk down' to us girls, but he was extracting yet another free meal out of us.

"My dress is more than suitable for Mr Conroy."

"I think," said Helen, eyeing me up and down, "that you should wear my new scarlet neck-ribbon," and before I could object, she ran off to her room.

Our rooms were at the extreme ends of a long

passageway, with a large window at either end. There was a wall of doors on one side, and the balustrade overlooking the staircase on the other. My room was directly opposite the staircase, whereas Helen's room was in a sort of cul-de-sac at the other end, and facing the room where the old furniture was stored.

As it was barely five o'clock, the passageway was far from dark. I followed Helen so quickly that I was in time to see her heals as she ran into her room. Then, just as I lost sight of her, I saw another figure walking in front of me. It was a small thin woman, wearing a dove-grey dress, matching bonnet, and a black tasselled shawl. Though she had her back to me, something in her gait told me that she was not young.

I called out, "Fanny, is that you?" Fanny was my mother's Irish maid, who was known to perform the odd practical joke, and as she was a young woman, not the least like the person in front of me, I thought she had dressed up to play a trick.

The figure took no notice of me, and to my utter amazement, disappeared into the storage room. I don't mean that she unlocked the door and entered. No, she just walked through the door as though it were not there.

Perplexed, I entered my sister's room. Helen was standing in front of her dressing-table, head down and searching for the ribbon.

"Oh, where did I put it? When I didn't respond she looked up. "Goodness me, whatever is the matter with you? You look like you're about to faint." When I told her what I'd seen, she looked rather startled. Nevertheless, she insisted that we search the room. "If she went in, then she must still be there, otherwise we'd have seen or heard her come out."

Determined to catch the miscreant, we stepped across the passageway. I grasped the handle and turned. It was locked, with the key on the outside as usual. It was Helen's turn to look perplexed, and naturally she questioned me at length, but I was adamant.

We searched the room from top to bottom. We even crawled under the bed, coming out the other side looking like chimney sweeps, but there was nobody else in the room and by all appearances, no one had been in it for weeks.

We barely had time to make ourselves presentable before the dinner-bell rang, and as we hurried down stairs, we agreed not to say anything about it in the presence of the servants. After dinner however, when we were in the drawing-room, we told the story. My mother and brother listened attentively, declaring that they were as puzzled as we were. Mr Conroy however, laughed uproariously, which made me dislike him even more.

We waited until he had gone before discussing it further. My mother did her best to find a plausible explanation. Was I sure it hadn't been a trick of the light, and that it was Helen whom I'd seen? My answer was instant and unshakeable.

"She doesn't own a shawl like that."

Was I quite certain it hadn't been Fanny carrying a shawl?

"I called out to her."

Finally, we called Fanny and cross-questioned her, but with no result. Moreover, she and the other servants had been downstairs in the kitchen at the time. Now, Fanny was smart, quick on the uptake, and we could tell by the way she was looking at us that she knew something was afoot. Fortunately, my brother came up with a reasonable explanation about a prowler, and asked her not to say anything to the other servants, lest they should be frightened.

For days afterwards, Helen and I could not stop talking about it. We even gave her a name, 'The Grey Lady'. Eventually, my mother lost patience, forbidding us to mention it further. Or at least, that's what she pretended. In reality, as I discovered many years later, she had written to our family doctor about it. He had advised her to put a stop to it, insisting that it would have a bad effect on our nerves, especially mine. Silly old fool, his advice was pointless, for I was more annoyed than frightened, annoyed because I could not solve the mystery.

The intrigue was soon overshadowed by another event. You remember the date – March, 1855? Does that mean anything to you? No? Then allow me to elucidate. It was the spring following the dreadful Crimean winter campaign. We were still in Ireland, and I had just received a letter from a friend, informing me that England was awash with gossip. The Czar was dead, and everyone was wondering and fearing what would happen next.

I was in my bedroom, reading the letter for about the fifth time that day, when I heard mother calling my name. I put the letter on a small table beside my chair, stood up… and froze. Standing between me and the door, was 'The Grey Lady'. She was looking at me inquiringly, her head tilted slightly to the side, as though wondering who I was, and what I was doing there. Her face was refined and pleasing, certainly nothing to alarm or repel, and her lips were slightly parted, as though on the verge of speech.

Conversely, no power on earth could have made me

speak, for it had dawned on me with an awful thrill, that this was no living being. I fell backwards into the chair, and covering my face with my hands, tried to collect my senses. After a while, I began to feel stronger, more sure of myself. I took a deep breath, uncovered my eyes, and rose to my feet.

Oh, the relief. She was gone. My terror however, was not quite at an end. I ran out of the room, and was on the point of descending the stairs, when my reason, and I am quite sure, my sanity, snapped. She was ascending the staircase, coming closer and closer in an attitude of greeting a guest.

The next thing I knew, I was in the drawing-room on the sofa, surrounded by my terrified mother and sisters. I could find neither voice nor courage to tell them what had happened, and for several days thereafter, fell seriously ill. Physicians today would call it a 'nervous breakdown', but in any event, I could not endure to be alone, even in broad daylight.

We vacated the house as soon as practicable. I was not sorry to leave it, and upon settling back into my old familiar home, horror and nervousness began to wane. Then, almost a year later, I was told a curious story, and many of the pieces of the puzzle, though not all, fell into place.

I was staying with one of my Aunts, and one evening, the conversation turned to ghosts. My Aunt, who of course was acquainted with my experience, urged me to recount the story.

At the conclusion, an elderly lady who was also a guest, astonished me by saying, "I think I can tell you whom you saw. Does the name Fitzgerald mean anything to you?"

"No, nothing."

"Then, allow me to enlighten you. The Fitzgeralds were once a great and wealthy family, but a series of misfortunes brought them low. The family gradually died out, until eventually, only three elderly sisters remained. Being spinsters, and with no kin to care for them, their pecuniary resources were virtually nil. They had no choice but to utilise their only remaining asset, the house."

I held up a finger to politely interrupt. "And this is where Captain Larchmont comes in, for it was he who rented the house to us."

"I am not acquainted with the finer details, but on the balance of probability, I would say that this was the case. I would also say, that being a gentleman, he allowed the sisters to store their bulkier possessions while they resided in reduced circumstances."

"The storage room," I exclaimed. "It was full of cabinets and other cumbersome furniture."

"Precisely. Afterwards, unable to bear the disgrace of such a fine name being reduced to little more than penury, the sisters moved to the Continent. But, if ever a heart was buried in a house, it was that of the eldest sister, Amelia Fitzgerald."

"And you think that's who I saw?"

"Yes, I think so. The description certainly fits. You see, Miss Amelia died in Paris in March 1855, her sisters having predeceased her."

"That was the same time that we were in the house. I wonder what happened to it."

"It was probably sold." She laughed. "Mind you, whoever owns it now, will probably find that they have one fixture not easily removed."

8
DOUBLE TROUBLE

Mr Walter Woolfield, had been a widower for twelve months. Since his wife's death, he had worn sober clothing, accepted a seemingly endless stream of condolences, and behaved in the manner expected of the recently bereaved. Privately however, he was ecstatic.

His wife, Dimity, had been a pilgrim in every respect. For years she had made her husband's life a misery, branding him a moral and religious pariah. Whenever he had indulged in a little light reading, or had deigned to laugh, or partaken of wine, or enjoyed the plethora of pleasures that were anathema to the pious, her disapproval was palpable.

Dimity would invite her like-minded friends to dinner, serving a delicious table, where self-indulgent righteous superiority flowed as freely as the apple juice. On these occasions, Walter would sit at the bottom of the table, trying to look interested in topics of which he had little or no regard. Subjects such as football, horse racing, and cricket, were strictly taboo, whereas politics and literature were acceptable, but only if they leaned towards the derogatory, rather than the constructive.

Conversely, whenever Walter invited his own friends to dinner, the 'bill of fare' would be bland and unappetising. He could have endured his wife's hypocrisy, had she not sat silently at the head of the table, drumming her fingers and looking bored.

On the anniversary of Dimity's death, Walter

83

discarded his dowdy clothing, donned a light-weight suit and bright yellow cravat, set his hat at a jaunty angle, and went for a walk in the park. Everything seemed brighter and sweeter and more alive, and as he picked a daisy and presented it to a child, he vowed that he would never again fall into the clutches of a shrew.

Philippa Moreland, was bright, attractive, and well-educated, and it took Walter but a short courtship to propose. On the evening she'd said 'yes', agreeing that a protracted engagement was not necessary, Walter returned to his home a very happy man.

Sitting in the drawing-room in front of the fire, he was in the process of envisaging a contented future, when he heard a familiar, disapproving 'sniff'. Slowly, he turned his head. White and almost translucent, the features defined by shades of grey, Dimity was sitting on the couch, her expression set in its customary scowl.

"And what, may I ask, do you think you're doing?"

"Doing?" he said in a strangled voice, shrinking back in his chair. "Why, my love, I am contemplating life without you."

"Do not pretend to lament my passing," she said wrathfully. "You were always crude and infantile." She raised her eyes and hands in supplication. "It is only by the mercy of God that I have returned to guide you." Walter felt an insane urge to giggle. In all likelihood, she'd been sent back because she was too sanctimonious, even for the Almighty. Her next words however, instantly erased his levity. "You will never lead that woman to the altar."

"Woman?" he stammered, running a finger around the inside of his collar. The room had suddenly become very warm. "What woman? Really, my treasure, you astound me."

"Do not lie! I know all. Though you be a poor excuse for a man, I will still watch over you. When you quit this mortal coil, provided you are repentant, there is a chance, albeit slim, that our earthly union will become eternal."

Walter gripped the arms of his chair. "Join…joined, forever?"

"Yes, but you will never revel in glory if you don't turn over a new leaf."

Walter perceived a tiny glimmer of hope. "My soul is not worth saving. I would not put you to such trouble."

"On the contrary, it is my duty as your wife. Now, turn out the lamps and go to bed. You know how disagreeable you are if you don't get enough sleep."

Walter knew from the set of her jaw, that for the time being, he had no choice but to acquiesce. "You are excessively kind," he said with a sigh.

Depressed and confused, Walter went upstairs to his room, his footfall sluggish and heavy. Even the fire in the bedroom grate seemed unsure whether to burn brightly, for the late Mrs Woolfield had viewed a hearty blaze as a frivolous waste of money. Climbing into bed, Walter was just about to turn down the lamp when he let out a stifled scream. Dimity was standing by the bed. Even worse, she was wearing night attire.

"What…what do you want?" he asked uneasily.

"My grave is uncomfortable and damp, and I am cold, bitterly cold."

Alive or dead, Walter thought she had never said truer words. "I am sorry to hear it."

"Good, then you won't object if I resume my marital rights."

Walter grabbed the coverlet and pulled it up to his

chin. "But…but dearest, you will draw all the heat out of me and I'll be laid up with rheumatics."

"Nonsense," she barked, inflexible as ever, and moved to her former side of the bed.

Walter saw only one means of escape. "I…I forgot to turn down a lamp," and with indecent haste, he grabbed his dressing-gown and fled downstairs.

Half an hour later, and fortified by a generous slug of whiskey, he returned to his room. He was disgusted by his submissiveness, and determined to have it out.

"Dimity, why are you here? What do you want?"

Her eyes were as black and as hard as two lumps of coal. "I will not permit you to marry again."

"But why?"

"Because you're married to me."

"But you're dead, lifeless, insubstantial. Why, if I sent messages to all your old friends stating that you had returned, I'd be locked up. Is that what you want – my humiliation?"

Dimity pursed her lips. "Miss Moreland is not for you. She is flighty, irresponsible, and unpleasant."

"Unpleasant?" said Walter indignantly. "Have you looked in a mirror recently?"

"You can hurl all the insults you like, that's just about your level of crudity, but the fact remains that I will haunt you until you give her up - goodnight." She snapped her fingers and the lamp went out.

Walter sank into the armchair by the fire, his head in his hands. He had never faced anything like this in his life, but there again, who had? A priest? A doctor? Perhaps he should obtain one of those strange magazines, the ones that heralded the power of séances and mediums to banish 'unnatural' entities. "Oh shut up," he murmured, as Dimity began to snore. How could he get a ghost to 'move on'? Was there an address to which he could apply?

When Walter awoke the next morning, his neck was stiff and his back was sore. It took him a moment to remember why he'd gone to sleep in the chair. Then slowly, reluctantly, he turned his head. The bed was empty.

His relief however, was short-lived. During a visit with Philippa later that day, his wife stood behind the unsuspecting girl, arms crossed and eyes glowering. Intimidated, the hug Walter bestowed on his fiancée, was perfunctory at best.

"What, no kiss?" said Philippa gaily, noticing his hesitancy.

Walter sniffed in an exaggerated manner. "I think I'm developing a cold," he said nasally, not daring to look behind her. "To be honest, I don't feel very well."

"My darling, let me kiss you better."

"No!" Although he loved Philippa passionately, with the virulent ghost of his wife standing not three feet away, intimacy was the last thing he needed. "I'm sorry dear," he said in a jittery voice. "Perhaps I'll return home and go to bed. I have a stinking headache." This much at least was true, and it stayed the truth for several days.

Each night when he retired to bed, Dimity would be waiting, mouth pursed and eyes glaring. "Give it up, Walter. You will never marry her."

Walter took to sleeping in his study. He would bank the fire, fill his pipe, and drink his whiskey. But even then he was not left alone. At intervals, Dimity would thrust open the door and wag an admonitory finger.

"Do not consider yourself engaged, Walter. As the

Minister said the day we exchanged vows, 'In sickness and in health. For better or worse'."

The first spark of defiance ignited in Walter. It was not her words as such though reminding him that they'd once been married was painful enough. Rather, it was the fact that she had dared to infiltrate a recognised male bastion – the study.

"Leave this room immediately," he ordered, "and do not enter again without my permission."

Walter paid dearly for the moment of rebellion. Dimity's persecution became so intense, that he began to lose weight. In the office, she would peer over his shoulder and criticise his work, thereby causing him to make mistakes. At the library, she would follow in his wake and pull books off the shelves, and after the third occurrence, he was banned from the library for a month. But it was the incident at his club, when she raised an old man's wig, floated it across the room, and placed it on Walter's head that finally broke his resolve.

He had no choice but to submit, and not daring to communicate directly with Philippa, he sent her a note via messenger, asking her to meet him at a theatre. It was certainly not an appropriate location in which to break an engagement. However, given the late Mrs Woolfield's abstemiousness, Walter felt sure that it was the only place where he could speak freely without his ghostly shadow.

They sat in a stall where Philippa chatted merrily. Unfortunately, the subject was their forthcoming wedding. Feeling a wretched coward, Walter stopped her.

"Philippa, my dear," he began, his eyes downcast, "please, there is something I must tell you. You will think me dastardly and cruel, and you'd be right, but I have no choice. I must terminate our engagement."

Philippa, who had been wafting a fan, stopped abruptly. "What on earth are you talking about?"

"Please don't assume that my affection for you has abated. On the contrary, it is stronger than ever."

"Walter, you're not making sense. If you love me, then why don't you want to marry me?"

Walter took a deep breath. Preposterous though the reason was, she deserved the truth. "I know this will be difficult to believe, but I am being haunted by my late wife. She allows me no peace, hounding me day and night. She believes we are still married."

To his utter bewilderment, Philippa threw back her head and laughed. "Oh, is that all? My darling naïve fiancée, I also am being haunted."

It took Walter several seconds to find his voice, and even then, all he could say was, "You are?"

"Absolutely," she said, her voice still full of merriment.

"Look here, Philippa, this is serious. She always had an iron will, and she will not let us marry."

Philippa fanned her now flushed face. "Defy her. Ghosts are very exacting, give them an inch and they'll take a mile."

"But how do you know this?"

"As I told you, I am also being haunted. Were you with her when she died?"

"Yes. She said she wasn't afraid because she was going to a better place. I cannot condemn her devotion to the Almighty. I only wish she hadn't been so obsessed with it."

"Ha! That, my darling boy, is your method of attack. Ask her why she's not in the so-called better place. Tease her piety, throw it back in her face, that's what I do with Norman."

"Who's Norman?"

"Norman is my ghost. He was a great admirer of mine who tried to court me. But I never liked him, never gave him any encouragement. On the contrary, I treated him mercilessly, but he was one of those self-assured, ignorance is bliss type creatures, incapable of taking a hint. His capacity to forgive, along with his piousness and abstinence were, I'm sorry to say, nauseating."

"Sounds like my wife," said Walter dully. "How did he die?"

"The most abominable ill-luck. He had just acquired a new horse, and was taking her out for the first time, when a rabbit darted across their path. The horse reared and Norman was thrown to the ground, breaking his back. When I received word that he was dying, it would have been cruel to ignore him, so went to see him. I might have felt sorry for him had he not declared that, 'even in the bosom of God', he would always be true to me. Naturally I did not think he meant it literally."

"And he haunts you?"

"Yes, but I have learned how to counteract his religiosity. When he starts to spout diatribe, I am appallingly rude to him and it shuts him up. He just stands there wringing his hands and sighing in lament."

"This is a most curious state of affairs."

Philippa took his hand and kissed it. "The fact that we are being haunted by our, and I use the term loosely, paramours, only shows how well-suited we are."

Walter smiled for what felt like the first time in weeks. "Thank you my darling. However, the problem still exists. How do we rid ourselves of this nuisance? We cannot spend our lives in a theatre."

"We must present a united front. Marry in spite of

them."

"Huh, you don't know Dimity. As miserable as my life was beforehand, it's even worse now that she's dead."

As the orchestra tuned-up and the lights began to dim, Philippa squeezed his hand. "Don't worry, my darling, I am not afraid of her. I have a plan. If I come to your house tomorrow, will she appear?"

"Undoubtedly. She is consumed by jealousy."

"So is Norman." Walter slowly turned his head. There had been something in Philippa's voice that spoke of mischief, but as the theatre was now in darkness, he did not see the smile dancing around her lips.

When the performance was over, they joined the throng of patrons outside the theatre, most of whom were either waiting for a cab or their private carriage. Climbing into a cab, Walter sat on one side while Philippa sat on the other. She looked at him curiously, her head tilted to the side.

"Why aren't you sitting next to me?"

"I can't."

Philippa understood immediately. She stood up, turned around, and addressed the empty seat. "If you do not leave this cab at once, I will sit on you."

"She's gone," said Walter in delight.

"Of course she has. I knew it was her because, as we left the theatre, I saw Norman loitering near the door. Those two don't realise it yet, but they're working in cahoots." Philippa suddenly giggled. "Dimity might have gone, but I bet Norman is running behind the cab."

It took ten minutes to reach Philippa's home, and the lovers took advantage of their time alone. Ordering the cab to wait, Walter escorted his now radiant fiancée to the door, kissing her passionately 'good night'. He returned to the cab, gave the driver his address, and climbed inside. No sooner had he sat down, when Dimity suddenly appeared. As the cab passed the gaslights, her cadaverous face was momentarily illuminated, revealing her stony face and furious eyes.

"How can you pander to that hussy, especially in public?"

It seemed some of Philippa's courage had rubbed off on Walter, for he jumped to his feet and said sternly, "You go too far, madam."

"Apparently not far enough. I will not permit this marriage. No matter how much you plan and contrive, I will stand between you as a wall of ice."

Walter sat back, crossed his arms, and sulked. He spent another restless night in the study, and although Dimity did not enter, he could not prevent her from knocking on the door and calling out her entreaties. Never overly religious, he nevertheless prayed that Philippa's plan, whatever it was, would work. It then occurred to him, that if the Almighty didn't want his ridiculous wife, then why should he help?

When Philippa arrived at the house the next morning, not only was she dressed in glaring colours, but her lips were a vibrant red. Walter looked at her in astonishment, but she quickly shook her head. "Where is she?" she whispered.

Walter indicated the drawing-room. "She was in there a moment ago. Where's yours?"

"Behind you. You should have heard his tirade when I applied rouge to my lips."

"Yes, I'd noticed. Why the...erm...costume?"

Philippa patted the lapel of his jacket. "All part of the plan. Let's go in."

The late Mrs Woolfield, was seated in Walter's armchair, her hands clasped so tightly, that the knuckles resembled tiny moons. Norman was also in the drawing-room. Aged in his middle 30's, he was tall and gaunt, with a melancholy expression and large sad eyes. He spied his fellow ghost, rubbed his spine where he had received the mortal injury, and made an awkward bow.

"I believe I have the honour of addressing a sister pilgrim."

Dimity's eyebrows rose in surprise, a faint wintry smile touching her lips. "Precisely so. And to whom do I have the honour of replying?"

Norman introduced himself and then asked, "And how do you find being dead?"

Walter and Philippa were standing by a bookcase, pretending to read an encyclopaedia of plants. Whilst they could only see and hear their respective ghost, it was not difficult to deduce the other side of the conversation.

"I suppose the same as you," said Dimity, though Walter thought he detected a note of uncertainty in her voice.

"Ah, yes," said Norman with a hint of superiority, "but I am here to fulfil a most melancholy duty," and he glanced at Philippa with loving eyes.

From the corner of his eye, Walter saw his wife bristle. However, before he could ask Philippa what Norman had said, he saw Dimity adopt a virtuous expression. "The same can be said of me." She also glanced across at the lovers, but rather than adoration, her eyes were narrow and spiteful. "I will not allow my husband to marry that…that woman."

Norman blinked. "I beg your pardon? Are you casting aspersions on my beloved? I disapprove of the match as much as you do, probably even more, but I will not have Philippa's reputation sullied by anyone, living or dead."

"Sullied?" Dimity laughed scornfully. "Why, you only have to look at her to see she's…what are you doing?" Norman had sat down in the opposite chair. "I did not invite you to sit down," she snapped.

"And I didn't invite your contemptible opinion, but I got it all the same. Besides, my back is hurting."

Over by the bookcase, Philippa spoke in a voice that was barely a whisper. "I can only hear one side of the conversation, but I think they're arguing."

"Same here," said Walter, equally quietly.

"Good. Now to rub salt into the wound. Take me to the dining-room." Unseen by the ghosts, Philippa and Walter slipped out of the room.

"What do you propose to do in here," he asked, closing the dining room door.

Again, Philippa lowered her voice. "Just act naturally, and don't be surprised by anything I might say." Aloud she said, "Do you like this room, Walter? Personally, I find it very depressing."

"I suppose it's a bit plain."

"Plain? Why, it's positively dowdy. No pictures of note, no wallpaper, and just look at the state of that carpet." She pointed under the table to where Walter had usually sat. The carpet was virtually bare, the result of his grinding feet at his wife's nagging and moralising. "I suppose," Philippa continued, "if we cut off the end, we can put it in a servant's quarters, that's about all it's good for."

Walter could have kissed her. Her astuteness was amazing. "Yes dear," he said, beginning to get an inkling of the plan.

She pointed to the only two pictures in the room - Deer in Winter, and, Dignity and Impudence. "These pictures are now passé."

"My late wife did not object to them."

"Well your coming wife does. If you are attached to them, you can hang them in your study. Otherwise, we'll give them to the vicar for his next jumble sale."

There was a sudden commotion on the other side of the door. "Oh no you don't!" Norman's angry voice penetrated the room. "I happen to agree with her. Those pictures *are* passé."

"I'll have you know that my father gave me those pictures as part of my trousseau."

"Which only goes to prove Philippa's point."

Philippa stifled a giggle. "Good, it's working, let's keep going." She raised her voice to be heard above the din, "and the condition of the china?"

"The best china was only ever used when Mrs Woolfield was entertaining. Sadly, some of it was broken over the past year. The soup tureen has lost its lid, and I am short of two vegetable dishes and a platter."

"And the glassware?"

"The best wine-glasses are fairly complete, so long as there is no more than 11 at dinner, but the decanters are in a bad way. I am sure my late wife chipped them deliberately."

"Do you have a cook?"

"Yes, but not the one I'd like to have. Sally was an excellent cook, but my wife considered her too pretty, and rarely allowed me to venture into the kitchen."

Philippa grinned. "Was she pretty?"

"In a homely sort of way, I suppose so. But it was her muffins and cakes that were tempting. Just before she died, my wife replaced Sally with Mrs Withers. Warts, hooked nose, stale breath an' all. Dimity was never a good judge of character."

Philippa held up a hand. "Have you noticed something?"

"No." But as soon as he said it, he understood what she'd meant. He looked at the door, his brow furrowed. "It's gone quiet."

Philippa nodded eagerly. "Yes, I know."

They tip-toed back to the drawing-room. There wasn't a ghost in sight. There was, however, a note on the table. Philippa picked it up, read it, and then collapsed into a chair, tears of laughter streaming down her face.

Walter took the note and read aloud, "We have departed to settle our differences. We might not return for some time."

Philippa rubbed her aching sides as she declared, "We are free! They will never return."

Walter swept her up in his arms. "You clever, clever girl. You used their particular brand of jealousy as a weapon."

"I had a feeling that if they met, their pride and pomposity would clash, and I was right. Both were besotted to the point that neither would allow the other to get the upper hand, even at the expense of their principals, something which, in our marriage, will never, ever, happen."

9
FORGET ME NOT

Anna Markal was the prettiest girl in the village. At every dance, fete, or fair she attended, and there were not too many in which she was absent, she would laugh and flirt coquettishly. With large brown eyes, flaxen hair, and buxom figure, she had everything a young virile suitor could want in a wife, including a modest dowry.

The man who finally won her hand, was Joseph Arler, a park-ranger and woodsman employed by the government. He was over six feet tall and powerfully built, and coupled with his russet hair and a rather high brow, his appearance was somewhat ferocious. But this was far from the truth, for in spite of his intimidating physique, he was a happy, smiling, gentle giant, who only saw the good in people.

The day before the wedding, Anna's mother was busy in the kitchen, preparing mounds of food for the feast, and dispensing pearls of wisdom. Anna however, was only half listening, for there was something weighing heavily on her mind. She dreaded becoming a mother. Indeed, many of the women in the village, had already dropped none too subtle hints about 'the pitter-patter of tiny feet', and the last thing Anna wanted, was to have her pleasure-loving life curtailed.

Unable to endure her mother's prattling, Anna made an excuse and left the house. Skirting the edge of the forest, her mind was so consumed with bitter thoughts of crying snivelling babies that it was only when she crossed a wooden bridge spanning a fast-flowing stream she realised where she was. Ahead, was a small neat cottage owned by a gypsy.

"Yes," she murmured in satisfaction, seeing a spiral of smoke rising from the chimney, "old Rosie will know what to do."

Rosie did indeed know. The obligatory silver having been exchanged, they sat at a table where she made Anna take a bite out of two red apples, and then cut them in half with a small silver knife. "Six," said Rosie, extracting the pips. "You would have had six children, three boys, three girls."

Anna shuddered. "Will it work?" she asked testily, as Rosie carefully laid the pips on a piece of paper.

"Oh yes, but in order to do so, you must pick up each pip, kiss it, and give it a name."

Anna drummed her fingers impatiently. Why hadn't the old woman simply given her a potion to drink? She followed the gypsy's instructions, announcing in turn, "Eleanor, Mary, Helene, Frank, William, and I suppose, Joseph." The latter was uttered, not out of any sense of love or duty, but because she couldn't be bothered thinking of another name.

Rosie folded the paper and held it out. "It is done. Go to the bridge and drop it into the stream." Anna made no secret of her eagerness to be gone. At the door however, Rosie called her back. "Make no mistake, mistress, the spell is irreversible."

Anna was in no mood for cautionary tales. On the contrary, all she could see before her, was a lifetime of fun and frivolity. She hurried to the bridge, tossed the paper over the side, and then ran home, her mind now completely focused on the wedding. She did not see the paper break apart as it hit the water, nor hear the six tiny 'sighs' as the pips sank beneath the surface.

Amidst raucous cheers and hearty congratulations, the couple took their vows. Anna, as she knew she would be, indeed, as she expected to be, was the centre of attention. They moved into a cottage overlooking the village green, and for several weeks thereafter, Anna lapped up the fuss. But the firmament of goodwill did not last, and three years later, while the marriage was convivial, it was far from the perpetual merriment Anna had anticipated.

Joseph was often away for days at a time, leaving Anna home alone. Bored and resentful, instead of preparing a hearty supper for a hard-working man, she would serve whatever came to hand. Moreover, the nature of Joseph's job, scrambling over rocks and traversing the thick woods, meant that more often than not, his clothes were torn or damaged. Instead of undertaking the repairs herself, as a good wife should, Anna sent the garments to be mended. It was only when a repair was deemed urgent, that she consented to use needle and thread. Even then, it was executed with such incompetence, that it had to be done again by a seamstress.

Anna's mother, no doubt in the belief that her pretty daughter would make an 'advantageous' match, as opposed to a 'good' one, had spared Anna's delicate hands and rosy cheeks from the rigours of housework, by teaching her basic and menial tasks. Consequently, if Anna had ever done a hard day's work in her life, it must have been performed under the cover of darkness.

To alleviate the tedium, Anna would visit friends and acquaintances, but here again she was thwarted. Whilst she was never turned away, she could not understand their disinclination to gossip, much preferring to cook and clean and care for their children.

Joseph's nature was as such, that he bore his pretty wife's defects amiably, quelling her grumbling with a joke, or sealing her pouting lips with a kiss.

This only made Anna even more shrewish, for to add to her perceived woes, Joseph was extremely popular, especially with the village children. They seemed to know when he was coming home, for no sooner had he turned the corner to walk across the village green, his huge axe resting against his shoulder, than those who were in the vicinity, would shriek in delight and run to meet him. Indeed, it was not uncommon for others, roused by the noise, to run out of their homes waving in greeting. The fact that Joseph always had nuts or almonds or sweets in his pockets, and would make the children leap, or catch, or scramble for the treat, had nothing to do with their love for the gentle giant.

Whilst Joseph reciprocated their love, he had one particular favourite. It was a little lame boy with a white, pinched face, who hobbled around on crutches. Joseph would sit on the bench, perch the lad on his knee, and with the other children surrounding him, would tell stories about the forest and its animals. Anna, looking out of her window, bitterly resented the attention given to the children.

One evening, after an especially enjoyable session with the children, Joseph entered his home and greeted his wife, his face beaming with joy. She did not express her vexation in words, but neither did she display any pleasure, and it was then that Joseph noticed for the first time, just how shabby his home was. No pot or pan evinced the slightest shine, the woodwork and shelves were covered in dust, while the lack-lustre windows were streaked with grime.

"Anna, why do you not knit my socks like other wives? It is a pity to waste money on inferior stock. Home-made is always better, for not only do they last longer, but knowing they had been made by you, would warm the cockles of my heart."

"It is you who waste money, throwing it away on sweets for those pestilent brats, and you dare speak of 'inferior stock'."

Joseph paused, gathered his courage, and said what was uppermost in his mind. "Why, after almost four years of marriage, are we still childless? I have heard it said, that a barren wife who tends an empty cradle, will soon have a baby to rock."

"I want no baby here," retorted Anna, slamming down for the third time that week, a plate of pickled herring.

Joseph was unusually quiet for the remainder of the evening, and long after Anna had gone to bed, he sat meditatively in front of the fire, silent tears sliding down his face. The next day, Anna was brought the tragic news, that her husband was dead. A woodcutter friend had found him in the forest, shot through the heart. His body was brought home and laid on the bed, whence it was subsequently placed in a coffin.

"Probably poachers," said the friend the following day, looking into Joseph's peaceful face with melancholy sadness.

"No," said Anna, her voice muffled by a handkerchief and racking sobs. Upon seeing the hole where Joseph's heart had once beat, the truth had hit her like a thunderbolt. Her selfishness had cost a man, a good man, the only person who had ever truly loved her, his life.

"If there's anything I can do," said the friend as he left the room, but Anna shook her head.

"No," she said again, her voice barely above a whisper. A neighbour had offered to keep her company, but Anna had refused. She would spend the last night that her husband was above ground, alone and repentant.

She wanted to remember as a form of punishment, how indifferent she had been to his wishes, how careless of his comforts, how little she had appreciated his cheerfulness and kindness, and perhaps more importantly, his forbearance. She recalled how Joseph would scatter nuts amongst the children, or dispense kind words to the elderly or the infirmed, or give sound advice to a headstrong youth.

Anna bent over and kissed his cold lips, the coffin casting a black shadow on the ground. She heard a stumping noise somewhere in the kitchen, followed by the door being timidly opened. It was the crippled boy on his crutches. Without waiting for permission, and seemingly uninhibited by the superstition associated with a corpse, he hobbled to the coffin and kissed his friend.

"We shall miss him," he said in a choked whisper. "He was like an uncle or a big brother to us. To some, he was the closest thing to a father they've ever known."

For the first time in her life, Anna wanted to hug a child, to ease his pain and administer comfort. The only reason she didn't, was because she didn't know how. "Yes," she managed. "So I understand."

Leaning on his crutches, the boy crossed the room again, paused at the door, and then looked back over his shoulder. "Goodbye my old friend," he said through streaming tears, and quietly closed the door.

Anna tried to pray, but once again, she did not know

how. Closing her eyes, she sat with her hands lightly clasped well into the night, waiting for she knew not what. She did not open her eyes again until the clock struck midnight. All was changed. The coffin was gone, replaced by a cradle complete with mewing babe. With its russet coloured hair and tiny delicate fingers, there was no doubting its parentage.

Anna stooped and with infinite care, held the child in her arms. Instantly, she entered a world full of love and happiness. A warmth she had never known before flooded her heart, so much so, that every vein tingled.

Then, just as tears of joy were running down her face, the child vanished and a voice inside her head said, "It is not yours. You threw it into the stream." Wild with desperation, she jumped to her feet and looked around, but all she saw was the coffin and her dead husband.

Anna shook her head. She must have been dreaming. Hungry and thirsty, she opened the door and entered the kitchen, but here again, all was changed. It was no longer night, and a little girl aged about 4 with shining flaxen hair, was sitting in Joseph's chair beside the fire.

The child raised innocent blue eyes and said, "Mother, Frank will be home soon, and I know he has something special to ask you."

Before Anna could answer, the front door was thrown open, and in walked a young man with fair hair and the beginning of a moustache, his features like the dead Joseph. Beside him, was a demure looking girl with sparkling green eyes and a rosebud mouth.

"Mother," he said, taking the girl by the hand and pulling her forward, "this is Imogene, the baker's daughter. We have loved each other ever since we were at school. Will you give us your blessing?"

Anna reached out her arms to embrace them, but just like the baby, they all disappeared. "No!" cried the voice in her head. "You threw them into the stream."

Unable to endure the nightmare, Anna ran outside to the kitchen garden. The pots of herbs and rows of neatly growing vegetables were exactly where Joseph had left them, but no sooner had she caught her breath when the scene changed again.

She was on a battlefield, where the acrid stench of gunpowder and smoke, caught at the back of her throat. Moreover, the roar of the cannon, and the rattle of muskets, barely drowned the screams of the wounded. Then, as a battalion of soldiers with bayonets affixed, charged past her, a red-headed man turned and smiled.

"Don't worry, mother, we'll beat them," he yelled as a volley of shots rang out. He died where he stood.

Anna screamed as a dense cloud of smoke rolled before her. She held her breath and waited, hoping against the odds that he was alive, but when an officer appeared and said, "Your son would have died a hero had you not tossed him into the stream," she fainted.

All was quiet when Anna staggered to her feet. She ran to the cottage, thrust open the door, and found herself in the midst of a poignant family scene. A middle-aged woman with reddish brown hair was lying in a bed, her head supported by a man who was clearly her husband. His face was wet with tears, and his eyes conveyed pure devotion, as did all the others, children and grandchildren, surrounding the bed.

"My darling Helen," he said tenderly, "I cannot express how much you mean to me."

A little girl holding a doll by the arm, burst into tears. She was ushered out of the room, but not before Anna heard her say, "Mama, please don't die."

A few minutes later, the father slowly rose from the bed, closed the dead woman's eyes, and carefully arranged her sweat-soaked hair. Anna felt her heart contract, her eyes brimming until she could see no more. She heard a church bell tolling in the distance, the resonating clang seeming to say, "This would have been your extended family, had you not tossed Helen into the stream."

Frantic with shame and sorrow, Anna ran blindly out of the house. She was now on the village green, but it was not as it ought to be, nor was it night-time either. To her utter astonishment, the sun was shining on a gleaming parish church. Built from an eye-watering white stone, the magnificence of its gilded spire was matched by the stained-glass windows. Moreover, flags were flying, flowers hung everywhere, and the people were dressed in colourful clothes. Clearly it was some kind of celebration.

"Sir Joseph has done his native village proud," said a man.

"Why do you call him 'Sir Joseph'?" said the elderly man standing next to him. "He is the son of a woodsman who was killed by poachers in the forest."

"Was he really?" said the first man in surprise. "I wonder if the Queen knew that when she knighted him. Sir Joseph is a great architect. I believe when he was a boy, he always had a pencil in his hand. You mark my words, when he is dead, there will be a statue erected here in his memory. In fact, it wouldn't surprise me if he designed it beforehand…but look, here he comes."

The crowd parted as a man with a high forehead, clear blue eyes, and a flowing white beard, made his way towards the church. He stopped every now and then, smiling and greeting those whom he recognised. And then his gaze fell on Anna. Their eyes locked for the space of two heartbeats, then just as before, the church bell chimed its mournful song and everything disappeared.

Dawn was just breaking when, sitting in the middle of the green, Anna howled like a wounded animal. Her cries soon attracted attention, and it was not long before she was surrounded by concerned people.

Anna, with a final scream of despair, flung herself forward and buried her face in the ground. She rarely spoke again. She didn't even attend Joseph's funeral. She now stands on the wooden bridge spanning the stream, where every day, instead of apple pips, seven bunches of forget-me-nots are tossed into the water.

10
THE WHITE WOLF

My name is Helmut Vogel, and I want to tell you a story. It is not a pretty tale, nor is it easy to tell, but I swear to you, with one exception which was born out of necessity, every word is true.

My father was an assistant game keeper on a large estate. With 300 acres of sprawling woodlands to patrol, keeping track of the deer, wild pigs, and other large animals, not to mention catching poachers in the act, was an exhausting job. He met my mother at a county fair, and after marriage, had three children in quick succession.

My parents had been married for about five years when tragedy struck. Late one evening, he mistook my mother for a poacher, and shot her. She did not die straight away, but implored him to flee with his children before he was arrested.

This he did, and I have vague memories of a long journey, of bitter cold and driving rain, and of seedy taverns and eating houses. Eventually, we settled in a one-roomed stone cottage, half way up a pine covered mountain. He could not have chosen a more secluded spot, for the nearest habitation was two miles away, and the nearest town closer to five.

A few acres had been cleared for cultivation, and in spring and summer, we grew vegetables to sustain us through the long harsh winter. We also collected great piles of wood, for, once the snow had fallen in earnest, the forest was virtually impenetrable. We did however, have a constant supply of fresh meat, everything from deer to wild rabbit.

Father had no one to assist him, nor to take care of us. This was more choice than design, for the tragedy of my mother's death, had left him shy of women.

Father was never happy unless he was active. He would go out hunting several hours every day, and fearful that during his absence we might come to some harm, he would lock us in the cottage. Also, he would not allow a fire in the big stone hearth. So, in order to stave off the cold, we would bury ourselves under a heap of animal skins, which were soft and furry and warmer than blankets, even if they did have a tendency to smell. When he eventually returned home, the reward for our patience, was a blazing fire and freshly cooked meat.

During the short daylight hours of winter, we would dream of spring, when the snow would melt, the woodlands regenerate, the birds return with their happy songs, and we would once again be at liberty. Such was our harsh, almost savage existence. Then, when Sigmund was 9, I 8, and Marcella 7, everything changed.

One afternoon father returned home later than usual. He was in a very bad mood. Winter snow had fallen in earnest, and he had only caught two skinny rabbits. He had brought in wood for a blazing fire, and we were blowing enthusiastically on the embers when, without warning, he caught Marcella by the arm and threw her aside. She struck her mouth on the leg of the table, and instantly knocked out a tooth.

Trembling with fear, she crawled into a corner, and, terrified of incurring further wrath, she used her dress to stifle her tears. Sigmund and I abandoned our task to comfort her, while our father drew his stool closer to the hearth. A cheerful blaze soon ensued, and although we three were shaking with cold and shock, we did not join him.

Such was our positions when, from very near the window, we heard the howling of a wolf, and as father jumped up and seized his gun, the howling came again, only this time it was more menacing and insistent.

"Wait here and keep quiet," he said gruffly, as though we had any choice in the matter, and in his haste to kill the wolf, he did not lock the door.

We all waited anxiously, for we thought that if he succeeded in shooting the wolf, he would return in better humour. While it was true he was harsh on all of us, especially Marcella, we loved our father dearly, and when he was happy, instead of severe, he was almost a different man.

After about half an hour or so, there was still no sound of a gunshot. "Father has followed the wolf into the hills," said Sigmund. "He won't be back for some time." He looked at Marcella's swollen and bloodied mouth. "Come on, we'll wash your face then sit by the fire."

By eight o'clock, father had still not returned. He was such a prodigious hunter, that it never occurred to us that he might be in danger. "I will look out and see if he's coming," said Sigmund, going to the door.

"Oh, do be careful," said Marcella. It was the first time she'd spoken since being cruelly treated, and her words were slightly slurred. "If there's one wolf about, there's bound to be others, and we have nothing to kill them with."

Sigmund opened the door just sufficiently to peep out. Even so, the icy blast embraced the room. "Nothing," he said after a time, and returned to the fire, his nose blue with cold.

"Nothing is right," I said grumpily, my rumbling tummy betraying my thoughts. "We haven't had any supper." Father usually cooked the meat as soon as he came home.

Marcella suddenly brightened. She was like a General directing the troops. "We shall cook it ourselves. Helmut, you and I will prepare the vegetables. There are some old potatoes in the sack by the door, just cut out the bad bits. Sigmund, you skin and chop up the rabbits. I think there's some venison left over from yesterday, so we can throw that in as well. When father comes home, after killing the wolf, he'll be doubly happy."

I glanced sideways at Sigmund, and like me, he was moved to tears. For such a tiny creature Marcella was showing a maturity beyond her tender years. But then, that was not uncommon in the mountains, where survival was a constant battle. We had watched our father prepare many meals, and it was not long before the thick iron casserole dish, which Sigmund had set before the fire, was filling the hut with the delicious smell of stew.

Suddenly, we heard the sound of a horn, and a few minutes later, father swung back the door. We stared in amazement. We were all expecting him to be carrying a wolf, but instead, he was preceded by a young woman in a long white cloak, and a dark swarthy man in heavy cloth.

At this point, I will relate what was only made known to me later. When father left the cottage, he saw a large white wolf about thirty yards ahead. Upon seeing father, the animal retreated slowly towards the forest. Growling and snarling, it did not run, and kept looking back over its shoulder as it travelled further into the woods.

Father did not want to fire until he was sure he would hit, thus the wolf led him a merry dance. The pursuit lasted for hours, and with the moonlight bouncing off the pristine snow illumination presented no problem. Sometimes the creature would leave father far behind, and then stop and wait as though to say, 'catch me if you can'. As soon as father came within range, the wolf would turn and run ahead, all the while ascending the mountain.

It is extremely rare for a mountain range not to have an area of superstition or evil attached to it, and ours was no exception. One of these areas, a small clearing where somewhat curiously, the trees refused to grow, had been pointed out to father by other local hunters, who all declared it 'dangerous'.

Perhaps he disbelieved the stories, or perhaps in his eagerness he forgot them, but in either event, the abominable creature led father to the clearing. It darted across to the other side, and then stood perfectly still and defiant, a ghostly echo of legends past.

It did not occur to father until much later, that there were no prints or tracks in the snow. Then, as he approached and raised his gun, the wolf suddenly disappeared.

Bewildered, he searched the clearing but to no avail. How could it have escaped without him seeing it? It was beyond his comprehension. He was about to start the long descent, when he heard a horn in the near distance.

Astonishment at such a sound, at such an hour, and in such a place, vanquished his disappointment. He remained riveted to the spot. Then, just as the horn sounded for a second time, a man leading a horse, with a woman slumped forward in the saddle, entered the clearing.

At first, my father recalled the strange stories he'd heard about supernatural beings allegedly frequenting the mountains, but as the pair drew nearer, he was satisfied that they were indeed, mortal. Even so, he kept a firm grip on his gun.

"What are you doing here?" he asked. "Who are you?"

"My friend, we have ridden far in fear of our lives. These mountains have enabled us to elude our pursuers, but if we cannot secure food and shelter, our flight will have been for nought. The strain and cold have already taken their toll, and my daughter is more dead than alive. Can you in some manner, assist us?"

"My cottage lies some distance away," replied father. "You are welcome to its shelter for the night. May I ask from whence you came?"

"From Quebec, where our lives were in equal jeopardy."

This announcement stirred my father's heart, for he remembered the tragedy which had forced him to flee, and immediately offered all assistance.

The man graciously bowed his head. "Thank you. It is no understatement to say that you have saved our lives."

Father began leading them down the mountain. "You are most fortunate. I was in pursuit of a large white wolf, otherwise I would not have been out at this time of night."

The woman spoke for the first time. Her voice was low and slightly husky, but as father later conceded, this was more likely due to the cold. "It ran passed us just as we came to the clearing," she said, "the vicious brute." About an hour and a half later, they entered the cottage.

"Apparently, we're in good time," said the man, breathing in the smell of rabbit stew, and not being delicate about it. He came to the fire and surveyed us in one glance. "You have good young cooks here."

"I'm glad we shall not have to wait," said father. "Come, mistress, sit by the fire."

We moved our stools in order to make room, but as the man was standing with his back to the fire, his coat steaming with melting snow, it was a tight squeeze.

"And my horse?" he asked. "Where can I put him?"

"I will take care of him," said father, and exited the cottage.

Under the pretext of stirring the stew, which was now so well-cooked that it had almost spoilt, I took the opportunity to have a good look at the woman.

She was young, about 20 years of age, and very beautiful, and when she pulled back the ermine trimmed hood, in the dancing flames of the fire, her flaxen hair resembled a wheat field. Her lips were full and intensely red, and her mouth, although somewhat large when open, revealed the most brilliant teeth I had ever seen. But there was something about her eyes, bright as they were, that was disconcerting, and I thought I detected a measure of cruelty.

She spoke kindly to Sigmund and myself, patting and caressing us with her slender pale hands. Marcella however, would not go near her, and when father returned and the supper served, she sat at the far end of the table.

When it was over, father insisted that the woman take his bed, while he and her father would sit by the fire. After what I now realise was token hesitation, she agreed to the arrangement. Sigmund, Marcella, and I slept together in the one bed as usual.

Having strange people sleep in the cottage, was a new experience for us, and when father produced some spirits, which he rarely drank, and he and the man began speaking in low voices, our ears were ready to catch every word.

"May I ask the cause of your flight?" said father.

"I was a servant to a most despicable man, and when he demanded that my girl surrender to his wishes, I gave him a few inches of my hunting knife."

"We are not only countrymen, but brothers in misfortune, for I too fled for my life."

"Do you realise," said the man with a light laugh, "that we haven't actually introduced ourselves? What is your name?"

"We now go by the name of Vogel, but it was formally Belmonde, and I am Pierre Belmonde."

I heard the sound of breaking glass. Then, as witnessed by the shadows that fell across the ceiling, the man jumped to his feet and embraced my father. "But…but this is marvellous, miraculous even. I know your tale as well as my own. I am your second cousin, Wilfred Fontaine."

After that, the conversation was conducted in excited whispers. All we could glean was that our new relative and his daughter, whose name was Christina, were to take up residence in the cottage, at least for the time being. A short time later, exhausted but elated, father and Wilfred fell asleep, snoring and grunting in unison.

"Did you hear that?" I whispered in Marcella's ear. "We're going to have company for a while. With a woman in the cottage, perhaps father will be a little kinder to us." I reached out a hand to stroke her hair, and despite the warmth of the animal skins, her tiny body was cold as stone.

"Helmut, I cannot bear to look at that woman. Every time I do, I feel very frightened."

"Everything will be alright," I said soothingly. "Go to sleep."

The harsh winter slowly drifted past, and with five people inside the cottage instead of three, it was severely cramped, and yet somehow, we managed to live comfortably. Father and Wilfred hunted every day, while Christina and we children performed the household duties. She was very kind to us, especially Marcella, whom she touched and indulged at every opportunity, and gradually, Marcella's dislike and mistrust of Christina, faded away.

The most notable change however, was in father. He seemed to have conquered his aversion to women, for he was most attentive to Christina. Often, after everyone else had gone to bed, they would sit up long into the night, conversing in whispers in front of the fire.

Wilfred and Christina had been at the cottage about a month, when one morning, we awoke to a splendid blue sky. The snow was still deep and the air bitterly cold, but just the sight of the watery sun lifted our spirits considerably. Dressed in fur-lined jackets and leggings, we frolicked and raced around outside, the sun making the snow sparkle like diamonds.

I could not control my laughter as Wilfred pulled me on a make-shift sledge. His strength and vitality seemed inexhaustible. "Come on, papa," I shrieked as we sped past the cottage. I shall never forget it. Father and Christina were standing in the doorway, his arm lightly resting around her shoulders. I had never seen him so content, and what's more, he was smiling. His features had hardened with the ruggedness of life, but at that moment, he was a very handsome man. Christina obviously thought so too, for later that night when we children were in bed, we heard the following conversation.

"So, you wish to marry my daughter," said Wilfred. "My blessing be on you both. I shall of course be sorry to lose her, but I take comfort that she is marrying a fellow countryman. Now that the matter is settled, I shall leave you and seek my fortune elsewhere."

"Why not remain here?"

"Thank you but no. Even a newly married couple of mature age, requires some degree of solace. Knowing my child is safe, is sufficient."

"I thank you for her, and will duly value her, but there is one difficulty. The nearest priest is some five miles away, and I doubt even the devil could lure him up the mountain at this time of year."

"And yet there must be a ceremony before I leave." Wilfred fell silent for a time, and then said, "Will you indulge me? Will you marry her if I choose the words? As her father, and with no other binding official to hand, it is not unreasonable that I should claim that right. If you are agreeable, I will marry you directly."

"I will," replied father.

"Then take her hand and swear the following. By all the spirits of all the mountains…"

"Wait, why not by 'heaven'?" interrupted father.

"Because I am not a priest, and we are not in a place of worship. Now, will you be married, or shall I take my daughter away?"

"Very well, proceed."

Wilfred cleared his throat. "Please, repeat after me. I swear by all the spirits of all the mountains, by all their power for good or evil, that I will take Christina for my wedded wife, that I will love, protect, and cherish her, and never raise a hand against her."

Father duly repeated the words. Wilfred then continued, "If I should fail in my vow, may all the vengeance of the spirits fall upon me and upon my children, may they perish by the vulture, by the wolf, or other beast of the forest, may the flesh be torn from their limbs, and their bones scattered in the wilderness."

As father repeated the last sentence, Marcella burst into tears. The sudden interruption discomposed the party, especially my father, for his censure was hard and cruel. Marcella buried her head under the blankets and continued to cry quietly.

Such were the circumstances of my father's second marriage. Christina had not uttered a word. The next morning, Wilfred expertly mounted his horse, which seemed unusually nervous, and after tearful farewells and promises of letters, they began to descend the mountain. No sooner had he departed than our trust in Christina was shattered.

Whenever father was away hunting, Christina would often beat us for the slightest misdemeanour. Her eyes would take on an eager, almost hungry look, and whenever Marcella remonstrated, so great was the grip, that my sister's thin arms were covered in bruises. Then, late one evening Marcella gently shook us awake.

"What's the matter?" said Sigmund sleepily.

"She's gone out in her nightgown, I saw her. She got out of bed, looked to see if father was asleep, and then crept out the door."

"You must have been dreaming."

"Look for yourself." We all raised our heads. Marcella was right. Only father was asleep in his bed.

We were all thinking the same. What could possibly

have induced her to go outside, especially this late and in such bitter weather, for winter had shown it had not finished yet. The answer, was a menacing growl near the window.

"It's a wolf," said Sigmund urgently, starting to rise. "Christina will be torn to pieces. We had better wake..." but his words were cut off by the sound of the door.

Still in her nightgown and completely intact, Christina noiselessly dropped the latch. She then went to a pail of water and washed her face and hands, and then slipped back into bed next to father. Minutes later, we heard the sound of rhythmic breathing.

I remember thinking that she was extremely brave to confront the wolf alone, but when the pattern was repeated over several nights, I began to suspect that her nocturnal sojourns, were not as they seemed. Sigmund, as I discovered, was of similar mind, and we determined to watch her closely.

Our observation revealed only one oddity. At meal times, she rarely ate the food on the table, but when she was preparing the raw meat for cooking, she would furtively cram a piece into her mouth.

Sigmund did not want to speak to father until he knew more, and was resolved to uncover the truth. Marcella and I endeavoured to dissuade him, but he was determined, and a few nights later, he came to bed fully clothed. As soon as Christina left the cottage, he jumped out of bed, took father's gun from the mantelpiece where it usually lay, and followed her out.

Marcella and I clung to each other, our hearts beating as one. A few minutes later, and some distance away, we heard the report of a gun. The door suddenly opened and Christina entered. I instantly clamped a hand over

Marcella's mouth, although in truth, I also wanted to scream. Even in the dim light from the fire, which had been dampened down for the night, it was easy to see that there was blood on Christina's nightgown.

Christina limped across to the fire, but in her haste to set it ablaze, she dropped the heavy poker. The noise caused father to stir. "Who's there? What's the matter?"

Christina spoke in her soft cooing voice, the voice reserved only for father. "Lie still, dearest, it's only me. I have lit the fire to warm some water, I am not feeling well." When she was sure father was asleep again, she tore off her nightgown to reveal a wound in her right thigh. She washed and dressed it, threw her nightgown into the fire, donned fresh clothes, and then sat by the hearth all night.

Where was Sigmund? How had Christina received the wound? Who fired the gun? Marcella finally fell asleep in my arms, but I lay awake all night. If Christina was aware that my eyes were riveted on her back she gave no sign of it. I was determined to speak first when father awoke, and when the hour duly arrived, I did.

"Father, where's Sigmund?" He knuckled the sleep out of his eyes, but before he could do or say anything, Christina let out a gasp of horror.

"Oh no! I was unwell last night, and being restless, I went outside for some air. I must have forgotten to lock the door." Her eyes suddenly flew to the mantelpiece. "Pierre, where's your gun?"

Father looked perplexedly at the mantelpiece, then seizing a broad axe, ran out of the cottage. He returned not ten minutes later, Sigmund's mangled body in his arms. He lay it gently on the floor, silent tears streaming down his face. I had never seen him cry until then.

Marcella and I flew out of bed, kneeling and wailing beside the body.

"He must have heard an animal during the night and taken the gun," said Christina. "Poor boy, he has paid dearly for our protection."

The latter was said with neither affection nor conviction. I wanted to speak, to tell all that I knew, but Marcella, perceiving my intention, pinched my arm. She looked at me so imploringly, that for her sake alone, I desisted. Although we could not comprehend it, we were conscious that somehow, Christina was connected with my brother's death.

Marcella and I watched from the door as father dug the grave. Brushing away his tears, which in the freezing air must have stung, he laid Sigmund to rest, a pillow of fine furs for his head. I could 'feel' Christina standing behind me, and not trusting myself to speak, I went across to help father. He was piling heavy stones on top of the grave, so that ravenous beasts would not be able to dig up the corpse.

The shock seemed to age father. He did not go hunting for several days, and would suddenly burst forth with cries of vengeance. On these occasions, Christina would sit quietly by the fire and pretend not to hear. Moreover, her nocturnal wanderings continued as before, but perhaps not as frequently. Eventually, the depletion of food drove my father outside. He was back within five minutes, and he was furious.

"Would you believe that the beasts have contrived to dig up my boy, and now there's scarcely anything left of him?"

"Indeed," said Christina. She changed the subject. "I need more wood for the fire."

Marcella looked at me, and I saw in her intelligent eyes, the encouragement to speak up. I chose my words carefully. "Father, I have heard a wolf under the window several times now."

"Wolf? Why did you not tell me this beforehand? Wake me the next time you hear it."

The days grew longer and the snow gradually abated, as did Christina's nocturnal ramblings. We ventured more and more outside the cottage, and as the ground became more workable, father turned his attention to vegetables. I was often called to assist him and Marcella would sit by us while we worked, leaving my step-mother alone in the cottage.

One day, father, Marcella and I, were planting potatoes, when Christina called out to say that she was going in search of some herbs, and that Marcella must return to the cottage and watch over the dinner.

"Do I have to?" said Marcella grumpily, her eyes following Christina into the forest. For an answer, I grinned and shoved her in the direction of the cottage.

About half an hour later, we were startled by a terrified scream. "Father, it's Marcella, she's burnt herself." We threw down our tools and ran to the cottage, but just before we reached it, a large white wolf darted out the door.

Marcella was lying prostrate on the floor, her savaged body awash with blood. She looked on us kindly as her life ebbed away, and then she looked on us no more.

Father and I burst into tears. We were still kneeling by the tiny body, when Christina returned to the cottage. I don't know which angered me the more, her words, or the fact that she showed very little emotion.

"Poor child, it must have been that great white wolf

that ran passed me as I came out of the forest. I assure you, Pierre, she's quite dead."

"I know she is!"

I thought my father would never recover. He mourned over the body for days, and in spite of Christina's constant urging, would not consign it to a grave. The onset of putrefaction forced him to yield. He lay her to rest close to Sigmund, and took every precaution against violation.

I lay alone and miserable in the bed we had shared. I felt sure Christina was implicated in both tragedies, but I could not account for the manner. There was only one solution. I must imitate Sigmund, and follow her.

As expected, Christina left the cottage. I silently counted to 20, then tip-toed to the window.

The moon was bright and the night still and clear, and I could see the graves of my brother and sister…and then I saw something else. I did not hesitate. "Father! Father! Wake up! Get your gun. Marcella's grave!"

"What? The wolves?" He threw on his clothes, grabbed his gun, and ran to the door which I had already opened. Imagine his horror when he beheld, as he advanced towards the grave, not a wolf, but his wife.

Christina was on her hands and knees, devouring Marcella with the avidity of a wolf. Father seemed to stop breathing, and I saw the gun begin to slip from his grasp. I grabbed the barrel and pushed it against his chest. The movement, or perhaps it was pure rage, restored his senses, for he raised the gun, took careful aim, and fired.

We stood for several seconds unable to move. The wretched woman jerked spasmodically. Then, as we slowly approached, she changed into a large white wolf.

"Yes, I see it all now," he said quietly. He spoke as though to himself. "It was she who, in the guise of a wolf, lured me into the mountains." He stood for a moment breathing hard, and then he said, "Helmut, fetch my axe." I did not argue, and by the time I returned, he had placed the remains of Marcella in the grave. I helped him re-build the mound, then he turned to me and said, "You do not have to stay and watch, but this I must do. I have not been much of a father, but at least I can avenge my children." When I nodded in ascent, he swung the axe and decapitated the wolf.

Early the next morning, we were aroused by somebody banging on the door. It was Wilfred, and his face was suffused with rage. "Where is my daughter? What have you done with her?"

"If there is any justice, then the fiend is where she ought to be, in hell. Now get out! I defy you and your power."

"Ah, but you have forgotten your oath never to raise a hand against her."

"I made no contract with evil spirits. Now I tell you again, get out."

Father seized his axe and swung it high, but it simply passed straight through Wilfred. The momentum sent father crashing to the floor. Wilfred laughed mockingly. "Mortal, we have power over those who have committed murder, and you my friend, are guilty of two. Your oath is registered, and you will pay the penalty attached to your marriage vow. Two of your children are gone, and there is one more to follow. But I am not in any hurry to exact full payment. For the time being, you will live with the knowledge of what you have done, and what is to come." He strode across the room, opened the door, and then turned to face me. Like Christina, his lips were red, his teeth were bared, and his grey eyes were ringed with yellow. "The world is a big place, young Helmut, but don't worry, when the time is right, I will find you."

11
THE DEMON DRINK

Devlin O'Riley was, as the saying goes, 'Jack of all trades and master of none'. Part grave-digger, part carpenter, part horse whisperer, he could fix a chair as easily as set a broken leg. To Devlin, it was simply a matter of application.

Aged somewhere in his 60's, he was well-spoken, honest and generous, which was why Squire Fallon employed him to minister to his hounds. The Squire lived in a fine old mansion, with woodlands and parks to please the most discerning of riders. It was also, according to local gossip, haunted.

Two generations earlier, old Squire Fallon was, according to the local peasantry, 'as good a gentleman who ever walked in shoes'. Indeed, his large portrait, above the fireplace in the study, depicted a man of noble stock, his bushy mutton-chop whiskers almost touching his collar.

The generous opinion of his character however, was not shared by his grovelling intimates, who behind his back, thought him ridiculous and overbearing. It was not his friendship they courted, nor did he have a pretty daughter with whom they could dally. Rather, it was an invitation to one of his house parties, or male only hunting weekends that they sought, for the old Squire was an inveterate drinker.

The manner of his death could not have been more appropriate, for he died from a burst blood vessel while pulling a cork out of a bottle. Since then, vast amounts of whiskey and wine had mysteriously disappeared within the study, with more than one valet sacked for alleged theft.

The current valet, Jimmy Talbot, had determined not to fall into the same trap, and every night for his past twenty years of service, he had locked all the liquor in a cupboard in the kitchen. He had just completed this tiresome duty when there was a loud knock on the door.

The wind was howling and the rain pouring, so that he had to grab the door to prevent it from smashing back against the wall. "What do you want?" he said testily, struggling to keep the heavy door in place.

Devlin stood on the doorstep dripping wet, a small dog wrapped in sacking in his arms. "A fire and quick," he said, disregarding the usual preliminaries.

Jimmy peered at the head resting in the crook of Devlin's arm. "That's Vixen isn't it? The Squire's best hound."

"Aye, but she won't be for longer if we don't help her."

"What's wrong with her?"

"She's whelping, but she's in trouble. She needs warmth and a tot of whiskey."

"Give a dog whiskey?" Jimmy was outraged. "Never heard of such a thing. Besides, the master left for Dublin this afternoon."

"I know that," said Devlin irritably, as the dog let out a pitiful whimper. "I am in charge of the hounds, and this poor mite needs help." He paused then added significantly, "If she dies, you can answer to the master, not me."

Although the two had never been 'friends', Jimmy knew enough of Devlin's character to honour the request.

"There has been a fire in the study all day. It will be warm in there."

"The study?" repeated Devlin in alarm, decades of subservience rising to the fore. "It would be most improper of me to sit in there. The kitchen will do just fine."

"If you don't want to wait while the kitchen warms up, then the study it must be."

Trying not to jostle the creature in his arms, Devlin cleaned his boots on the boot scraper by the door, and then stepped inside. The study was indeed still warm. Devlin lay the dog by the hearth, while Jimmy went to retrieve the restorative. He returned to the study with two glasses, a small jug of water, and half a bottle of whiskey, though not the best brand. He lit an oil lamp as Devlin forced a few drops of whiskey down the animal's throat, and a few minutes later, though listless, the dog was breathing easier.

"I'll have to stay with her," he said in a tone that declared he would brook no argument.

Jimmy banked-up the fire and then poured two glasses of whiskey. "Here," he said, handing Devlin a glass and pointing to an armchair by the fire, "we might as well make ourselves comfortable."

The two men talked for several hours until Jimmy fell asleep. Devlin was loathe to wake him lest he should shuffle off to his bed, for throughout the evening, his gaze had repeatedly wandered to the portrait above the fireplace, and he did not fancy being left alone. Was it his imagination, or had the proud and authoritative expression on the old man's face, changed to a sneer?

Devlin began to pace the room, a prayer poised on his lips, but no matter from which point he viewed the portrait, the eyes seemed to follow him. Such was his unease, that when the hound suddenly yelped in pain, he almost jumped out of his skin.

"Ridiculous," he muttered. "It's just my imagination." He took a stiff pull from the bottle of whiskey, settled himself in the armchair, and went to sleep.

It was the acrid smell that woke him up, and in the split second before opening his eyes, Devlin thought that the dog's fur was singeing. It took all of his courage not to scream. Standing before him, his eyes locked on the bottle of whiskey, was old Squire Fallon. Ignoring Devlin, who was quaking from top to toe, the Squire grabbed the bottle, smacked his lips, and drank.

"Ahhhhhh." His long moan of satisfaction, equated to a man who had just escaped dying of thirst. "Nectar of the gods."

Devlin found his voice, his manners, and most of his faculties. He stood up, bowed, and moved away from the chair. "At your service, sir."

"Who are you?" Devlin introduced himself. "Ah, yes, I think I remember you. You were a respectable man, industrious and sober."

Devlin had been 18 years of age when the old Squire had died, and whilst he was sure that the assessment of character, though accurate, did not pertain to him personally, he was not about to argue the point. In fact, he thought it prudent to play along, though he was puzzled as to why Jimmy hadn't also awakened.

"Thank you, sir. You were always a civil gentleman, bless your soul."

"Bless my soul? Why, you presumptuous cur, where are your manners? I might be dead, but it's not for the likes of you to remind me of it."

"Beggin' your pardon your honour, I am an ignorant man." Although Devlin resented having to demean himself, there was always a chance that if they kept talking, Jimmy would wake up. Whilst he, Devlin, didn't want to terrify the old valet, the presence of another witness might persuade the spirit to leave.

"You most certainly are," said the Squire. "In my day, people knew their place. I was a kind and sober master, at least, as sober as most gentlemen, and while it is true that I did not always observe the Sabbath, I was charitable and humane to the poor."

Not having the slightest notion where the conversation was heading, Devlin could only comment, "Most Christian of you, sir."

"Christian?" he repeated scornfully. "It seems all my good deeds counted for nothing, for I am not where I expected to be."

"And mores the pity," said Devlin, suppressing a grin. "Perhaps your honour would like to have a word with Father Murphy? I'm sure Jimmy would be willing to fetch him."

"Hold your tongue you miserable blaggard. It's not my soul that needs fixing, it's my leg." He sat in the chair and stuck out a black boot. "It's never been the same since Rapier fell on me."

Devlin remembered the horse, for it was one of the first he'd trained. After the accident, it was put about that the horse had been startled and thrown the Squire over a fence. The truth, when it finally emerged, was very different. The horse had refused to jump the fence, and in a fit of rage, the Squire had whipped it mercilessly. The horse, in pain and fright, did jump the fence, but had stumbled upon landing on the other side. Though the animal had only suffered minor injuries, the Squire was not so lucky, and with his dying breath, ordered his stable manager to 'take a gun and shoot the brute'.

Devlin felt sick just thinking about it. "Perhaps it's some sort of reminder about what you did."

"Of course it's not! How dare you suggest such a thing. I have no regrets about anything. No, it's just that...well, where I am now, there's an awful lot of walking to be done. The constant hot weather is extremely unpleasant, and it's my...erm...lot, to fetch and carry water." He looked at Devlin appraisingly. "You appear to have good hands and strong shoulders. Perhaps if you give the leg a good pull, it'll bring it back into shape."

Devlin was so mortified, that as he stepped away, he almost trod on the dog. "Oh, please, your honour, I wouldn't dare touch you."

"Nonsense. Do as you're told." When Devlin still hesitated, the Squire added menacingly, "If you don't, then by the infernal regions, I will crush your bones to powder." Realising that he had no choice, Devlin took hold of the leg. "I think I'll just have a little nip to kill the pain," said the Squire unconvincingly, and licking his lips again, poured some whiskey into a glass and added a splash of water.

His scream was enough to wake the dead. It certainly roused Jimmy, who jumped to his feet just as Devlin was hurled across the room. The old Squire clung to the whiskey as though it were the last he would ever taste. But even as he desperately tried to drink, thick smoke and leaping flames had already engulfed his body. There was a tremendous roar, the dog yelped, and the Squire was sucked up the chimney.

"Are you alright?" asked Jimmy, helping Devlin to his

feet.

"It was the old squire...he was here," said Devlin, stammering like an idiot.

"I know," said Jimmy with a grin. "Not a bad bit of acting if I say so myself."

Devlin looked even more confused. "You were awake?"

"Of course I was. Forgive me, my friend, but the master and I have been trying to get rid of that devil for years, yet no matter what trap we set, he always outsmarted us. Then, when you arrived demanding whiskey, it occurred to me while I was in the kitchen, that I would try something else."

"I don't understand."

Jimmy held up the small jug of water. "Blessed by Father Murphy himself. Admittedly he gave it me some time ago, but it'll never lose its potency. It was in a bottle in the kitchen, but it's now in this jug."

Devlin slapped his forehead. "Holy water! You clever man."

Jimmy started to laugh. "Not as clever as her," he said, pointing to the blanket where the hound and seven puppies were resting peacefully.

12
THE POWER OF CREATION (1904)

Joseph Dawson was not a happy man. Outwardly, he was charming and affable, respectable and respected. He was rather handsome with fair hair and hazel eyes, and those who knew him would have said that he was a man with 'good prospects'.

It was his position as a solicitor's clerk that was making him uneasy, for he was aware of a growing restlessness that ran contrary to his principles. He had adopted the legal profession, not from any sense of justice, but at the request of his widowed mother, thereby following in his father's footsteps. Although Joseph had acquiesced, his dedication to the vocation was less than enthusiastic, for in spite of his retiring manner, he was the possessor of a vivid imagination, and the concentration required to process legal documents was stifling his creativity.

To compensate, Joseph would spend hours penning letters to his mother, who lived some fifteen miles away, describing in colourful prose, the antics and foibles of his employer, who had the unfortunate name of Mr Swindler.

Mr Swindler was a venturesome speculator. He, Joseph, had no reason to suppose that there was anything dishonest about it, but he did wonder whether Mr Swindler's access to trustee funds, might not reach the point of temptation.

Joseph had one more reason for discontent. He had lost his heart to Miss Astoria Vincent, a young lady of breeding with a small fortune, and to whom Mr Swindler was guardian and trustee.

Miss Vincent was tall and slender, with shining blonde hair and a sweet serene face. Like Joseph, she was rather bashful, and was unconscious of her personal, not to mention pecuniary, attraction. She moved in the best society, and much to Joseph's constant chagrin, would in time, he assumed, be married-off to some obscure knight.

Whenever Miss Vincent visited the office Joseph, with heightened colour, was always quick to offer her a chair. But their conversation never passed beyond generalities and whenever they met accidentally Joseph never advanced beyond civility, in that he would raise his hat and remark on the weather.

It was the stimulus of unrequited love that drove Joseph to write a romantic novel. Apart from changing location and names, he took his characters directly from life, with Astoria portrayed in all her perfections. However, he did not conclude the novel with a happy ending, for try as he might, he could not give his fictitious Astoria, a husband.

For Joseph, the hardest part of the book was the title. He would have liked to use 'Pride and Prejudice', as it fitted the personalities of the characters exactly, but that was already taken, so instead, he chose the simple if ambiguous name of 'Indulgence'.

Unconscious of its deadly accuracy, to Joseph's surprise, he found a publisher relatively quickly. Mr Chambers was shrewd and discerning, and recognised the author's ability.

"It won't appeal to the general public," he said during their interview. "It doesn't contain any blood-curdling scenes, no hair-raising adventures, nor spice or titillation to suit vulgar tastes. However, there are still those who prefer good, honest, uncomplicated work, which yours most certainly is." He then offered £50 for the story and all its rights.

Joseph was ecstatic. That he, who had never done anything bold in his life, should be an author! He accepted the offer with alacrity, but made one stipulation. The book was to be published under a pseudonym. Mr Chambers had agreed, and after considering numerous connotations, they finally settled on the name Giles Astor.

The first indication that anything was 'wrong' occurred shortly after publication. Joseph lived in a small but respectable boarding house, run by a somewhat dour faced widow, Mrs Brown, whose only failing as a landlady was a lack of culinary ingenuity. With the merest of greetings to the flabbergasted landlady, Mr Hedthrop, the local magistrate, burst into the house and demanded, "Where is he?"

Mrs Brown clutched at her throat. Clearly the magistrate, who it was well-known preferred improving his golf handicap to sitting on the bench, was in the foulest of tempers. "Who?" she stammered.

"That black-hearted villain, Dawson, that's who." He paused in his peregrinations to look at her. "You don't know, do you?"

"Know what?"

Mr Hedthrop produced a copy of 'Indulgence. "Here, read chapter 2. Now, where is he?"

Confused, Mrs Brown took the book. "Up the stairs and turn right, second door along." A minute later, there was another crash as Mr Hedthrop burst into Joseph's bedroom.

"What is the meaning of this?" he boomed, his

moustache bristling with indignation.

In addition to being a magistrate, Mr Hedthrop had served in the army, though to judge from his intellectual capacity, he could not have been a great asset. A martinet of the superior kind, the only thing that irked him more than disorder, was the fact that he had not yet received a knighthood. Joseph, who had been in the process of dressing, was well aware of the magistrate's proclivities, after all, he'd put them in the book.

"I beg your pardon?" he said, fumbling with the buttons on his trousers. "To what do I owe this honour?"

"Honour! How dare you speak of honour? You wrote that travesty called Indulgence. You, sir, are Giles Astor."

"I'm sorry, sir," said Joseph, feigning surprise, "but I have no idea what you're talking about." Then, to his horror, he saw his own copy lying on the bedside table. He moved across to the bed and began straightening the coverlet, hoping to thrust the book between the sheets, but it was too late, Mr Hedthrop had already seen it.

"Why, there is the very infamy by your bed."

"I certainly admit to reading it, but as for writing it…"

"Do not assume an air of innocence with me. Everyone in Lytton-Under-Lyne knows you wrote it. I don't object to your writing a book, any fool can do that, but what I do object to, is my inclusion."

"Really, Mr Hedthrop, you have no justification for such an accusation. The book does not bear my name. Besides, the golfing magistrate is named Headland."

Mr Hedthrop turned scarlet, his cheeks quivering with rage. "The name is irrelevant. That person is me, and you have irreparably corrupted my character. I have a good mind to ask Mr Swindler to prosecute you for slander." He paused as though regretting the suggestion, for there was a degree of dubiousness attached to Mr Swindler's character. He pandered to the gentry, was a self-righteous trustee, and was a financial consultant to businesses and the middle-class. In times of difficulty, he would offer his more regarded clients a loan to stave off financial embarrassment, with land or property as security, which ultimately passed into his hands. He was never 'seen' to be doing anything illegal, yet it could not be asserted with total confidence, that his honesty and integrity were above reproach. Mr Hedthrop quickly went on, "How can I possibly play golf after this? Why, I'd be a laughing stock, and I'm not the only one. I have no doubt that you will receive other complaints. Good-day to you." With that, he exited the room, stumped down the stairs, and slammed the front door.

Joseph began to pace the room. This was a situation he had not envisaged. He needed time to think. He needed breakfast. Yes, that was it, he always thought better on a full stomach. Arriving in the little dining-room however, his perturbation was further exacerbated, when the landlady appeared and slammed down a plate of bacon & eggs.

Mrs Brown had been a widow for over ten years. She was so short in stature, that had it not been for the streaks of grey in her hair, she might have been mistaken for a child.

"Why, Mrs Brown, whatever is the matter? Have you broken another dish?"

"You have taken my character and changed it into something else."

"I never did such a thing."

"Oh, yes you did. Mr Hedthrop was kind enough to show me your book."

Again, Joseph feigned ignorance. "My book?"

"You might have used the name Mrs Brooks, but I'd recognise my own character anywhere."

Joseph decided to capitalise on the fact the Mrs Brown had not named the book. "Surely if there is a landlady in the book of which you complain, she is fictitious."

"It is not a work of fiction, it is a work of fact, and a cruel fact at that. What has a poor widow like me got to boast of except her reputation? I'm sure I have never done anything hard by you, not even over fried your eggs. You have brought shame to my good name." She broke into a paroxysm of tears and ran out of the room.

Joseph felt numb, wretched, cowed. He pushed the bacon around on the plate, his appetite having vanished. All he had done, was use real people, albeit under different names, in a fictitious story. But then, perhaps that was the problem. Like oil and vinegar, the two did not mix.

He was distracted by a slight commotion outside. He went across to the window, but at the last moment, instinct warned him to hide behind the curtain. Three men were standing on the doorstep. Joseph recognised the rat-like features and quick darting eyes of his employer, Mr Swindler, immediately. The second was a young man several years older than Joseph, a Mr Baxter, while the last was arguably the more formidable of the three.

The Reverend Bartholomew Syner, pronounced 'sigh-ner', but which the local wags changed to 'sinner', was an assertive yet stoic man. His propensity for putting the fear of god into his parishioners, as though the almighty was about to unleash wrath and vengeance, was magnified by an extraordinary set of mutton-chop whiskers. Grey and bristling, rather than human hair, it looked like he had two ferrets stuck to his face.

His church, located in the centre of town, was an imposing structure built from solid stone. It was refreshingly cool on hot summer days, but damnably cold in winter. The services were long and dismal, for the vicar had a penchant for preaching rambling sermons, and for the singing of lesser known hymns, the words to which, many in the congregation could only give lip-service.

Mr Baxter was cheerful and amiable, and lived with his mother and three sisters. When it came to tennis, croquet, billiards, or cards, he was recognised as one of the best in the district. His expertise was garnered by the single motive that he had absolutely no inclination to work, a fact not lost on his long suffering mother. To keep the peace, he would occasionally stroll into town to seek employment. But, as he always 'regretfully' reported, it seemed Lytton-Under-Lyne had few openings for an enterprising chap.

Still sniffing, Mrs Brown entered the dining room. "There are three gentlemen outside waiting for you. They say they won't go away until you come out."

"I know," said Joseph as she shut the door. He waited until she went upstairs to make the beds, as she usually did, and then escaped via the back door.

He made his way to the river where there were blooming flower-beds, pleasant walks, and benches. Of primary concern however, was that it was not likely to be frequented at that time of the morning. He had half an hour to spare before he was due at work, where he could hardly avoid Mr Swindler. It was, so Joseph reasoned, better to confront his employer alone, rather than with others who also harboured grievances.

Joseph sat on a bench and began to think. He had been

the instigator of serious embarrassment, but what to do about it? Perhaps if he returned the £50 to Mr Chambers, he would withdraw the book. But no. The publisher had been to considerable expense for paper, printing, binding, and advertising.

Lost in his thoughts, it was a few moments before Joseph realised that he was not alone. Astoria Vincent was standing before him. Joseph jumped to his feet and removed his hat. "An early promenade, Miss Vincent?" he inquired politely. He then noticed that, instead of her usual vivacity, she was standing in an attitude of listlessness, and that her eyes were uncommonly dull.

Joseph was puzzled. Surely she was not offended. He had made her the heroine of his book, portraying her as the highest ideal of an English lady. He had been very careful not to cast a shadow over her character or abilities, 'painting' her exactly as she was.

"Mr Dawson, although accidental, I am glad to have met you where we cannot be overheard. I have something I must speak to you about, to wit, a great injury."

Joseph bowed. "At your service, madam. What may I do?"

"You can do nothing, the damage is already done. Not only did you put me in your book without my permission, but you took outrageous liberties with my character."

Joseph sighed heavily. There was little point in continuing to deny authorship. "You recognised yourself?"

"Of course I did. I stand before you a shell of my former self."

Joseph felt an unaccustomed pang of annoyance. As much as he adored Astoria, she was being overly dramatic. "Surely you exaggerate the case."

"On the contrary. It is extremely difficult to alter another's perception, particularly in regards to personality. You may have thought you were flattering me, but in creating your naïve and innocent heroine, you have omitted vital parts of my character, namely, my intelligence and rationale. In short, you have branded me a scatterbrain." She held up a hand when Joseph started to protest. "No, please do not attempt to justify your actions. I shall now be prey to any adventurer with a mind to seeking a fortune. Be assured, Mr Dawson, that should we meet again, no matter the circumstances, I will not know you – good morning."

Joseph buried his face in his hands. "What have I done?" he murmured through his tears. "How could it have gone so wrong?" He heard the town clock strike the hour but did not move. He could not face another day of mundane legal documents, not even to appease his mother. His mother? Yes – that was it. He would quit Lytton and stay with his mother, at least until he could find a solution.

If Joseph thought his day could not get any worse, he was wrong, for when he returned to his lodgings, his visitors were still waiting. The three men turned to face him as one. The vicar clasped his hands and closed his eyes, as though praying for patience. Mr Swindler's face was crimson with rage, his beady eyes darting maniacally, while Mr Baxter, his thumbs hooked into his waistcoat, looked ready for a fight.

"I know what you want," said Joseph. "For pity's sake, do not attack me en masse. One at a time please."

"Mr Dawson," said the vicar as he followed Joseph into the little dining-room, "this is a most serious matter."

In spite of his predicament, Joseph did not neglect his

manners. "Please, sit down."

"No, thank you, I speak more effectively when standing, or at least, I used to. By putting me in your book, you have destroyed my power of oration. I have been despoiled of my highest, noblest, most spiritual office. What my sermons will now consist, I dare not think. I may be able to string some texts together to form a lesson, but that is mere mechanics. I, the vicar of Lytton-Under-Lyne, have been reduced to insignificance. Moreover, cruel unthinking young man, my prospects for advancement in the diocese, are at an end." Seemingly satisfied that he had stated an incontrovertible fact, the vicar condescended to bow as he took his departure. "I shall send Mr Swindler in next. Good morning to you."

The solicitor entered like a whirling dervish. He tossed his hat onto the table with such force, that it skidded across the top and fell off the other side. "Mr Dawson," he began vexedly, "this is a scurvy trick you have played on me. You have painted me as an unscrupulous ne'er-do-well, and by no process, legal or otherwise, can it be erased. Fact notwithstanding that you had the gall to name the character, Mr Crook, my competency will be tarnished for years. I also need hardly add…you're fired!" He retrieved his hat, rammed it onto his head, and stormed out of the room.

The last to enter was Mr Baxter. His tone was not as severe as his predecessor, but not by much. "Sir, you put me in your book and portrayed me as a cad. Thanks to your interference, I am being bullied by my mother and sisters. Indeed, my allowance has been cut by half. If duelling were not outlawed, I would demand satisfaction," and with a haughtiness that would have been at home in any royal enclosure, he turned and left the room.

With aching heart and heavy tread, Joseph trudged up the stairs, packed his belongings, said a miserable 'goodbye' to Mrs Brown, and caught a train to his mother's.

When Mrs Dawson opened the door, one look at her son's expression and three suitcases, told her that something was terribly wrong. Nevertheless, she did not immediately press for information, for which Joseph was extremely grateful, and three days later, whilst partaking of afternoon tea in the drawing-room, he decided to come clean.

"I wrote a novel, a good novel at that, and it was published."

Mrs Dawson was both shocked and surprised. Shocked that her son had actually done something bold, and surprised because he hadn't sent her a copy. "Really? Why am I only hearing about it now?"

"Because I didn't have time to tell you before...before the trouble started." When Mrs Dawson genteelly folded her napkin, Joseph knew he had her full attention. "The problem, is that although the story is fictional, I based the characters on real people."

"And they recognised themselves?"

"Yes."

"My dear, I do not profess to be an expert on the subject, but a perusal of even the most mundane novel would have shown you that you never use real people as characters, unless it's some sort of biography. Why didn't you use your imagination? It's certainly fertile enough, and I cite your letters as proof of that, for they are always colourful and inventive."

"I just thought it would be easier to use real people.

You see, I was well acquainted with their personalities, their likes and dislikes, their foibles and weaknesses."

"Too well it seems." There was a short pause, and then Mrs Dawson asked unexpectedly, "When did you last visit the theatre?"

"Months ago. A comedy I think."

"Can you remember any of the characters?"

"Some of them – why?"

"Indulge me. Describe one or two."

Joseph began to think. "Well, there was a doddery old vicar who kept losing his glasses. Then there was a cook who couldn't really cook. Her best dish was tapioca pudding, which kept turning up in desk drawers and plant pots." He started to laugh. "Then there was an eccentric old Aunt who constantly carried a goldfish bowl." Joseph suddenly stopped, his expression rather dazed. "That's it…That's it!" He swept his mother up in his arms and danced around the room. "Mother, you're a genius. That's the answer…write another book!" He was giddy with happiness, so much so, that he almost ran out of the house without his hat.

"Where are you going?" his mother called out.

"To buy paper and ink. I have a novel to write!"

Joseph worked on the manuscript day and night, taking meals in a makeshift study his mother had organised, sometimes forgetting to eat at all. His only day of rest was Sunday when they attended church, but even then, he could be seen scribbling in a notebook.

His enthusiasm was given a further boost when, via Mrs Brown, he received a letter from Mr Chambers, stating that 'Indulgence' had sold better than expected, and that he would be pleased to consider a second novel, and with more liberal terms.

Joseph finally put down the pen. He looked at the neatly written manuscript with a peculiar sense of emptiness. On the one hand, it was finished, but on the other, it was a case of 'what do I write next?' While it was true that a character might have a passing resemblance to someone living, after all, nobody was THAT unique, of one thing he was absolutely certain, all the characters were entirely of his own creation. Nor did the title present a problem. As the story was a romantic comedy spanning a year, it had the simple name of, 'A Farce for All Seasons'.

It was about two months later when the postman knocked on the door. In his hand, was a brown paper parcel tied with string. Joseph's heart began to race, for he knew exactly what the parcel contained. Impatient to cut the cord and smell the freshness of the ink, to feel the crispness of the pristine paper, he hurried to the make-shift study. But no sooner had he closed the door, when he saw that he was not alone. Six people were seated around the table, or more accurately, six entities. Somehow, his creations had come to life.

At the head of the table, sat the good-hearted but slightly eccentric, Lady Winifred Carstairs. She was one of those aristocratic old ladies who, although appearing to be absent-minded, could be unexpectedly wise in times of crisis. She was also Virginia's Aunt.

Virginia was the heroine. She was daring, winsome, and not a little boisterous. She was also somewhat unconventional, in that she was brutally honest, which in the story, had led to hilarious situations. Next to her was the hero, a bright and vigorous young man, full of good sense with a high degree of culture.

Perhaps the 'oddest' person in the room, was the cook,

a happy, pink-cheeked woman, who was stirring a bowl of batter. "I've never met a family yet who didn't enjoy my plum duff." It was a direct quotation from the book.

Next to her, was the character of whom Joseph was the most fond, a white-haired lawyer, who enjoyed a joke, was able to tell a good story, and was scrupulous in all legal and financial matters. Last but not least, was the vibrant and audacious stockbroker, a man of sharp intelligence and quick determination.

Joseph stared in amazement. He felt no fear, but rather a sense of pride. "Good morning," he said, beaming. But after his greeting had been acknowledged, he found that he didn't quite know what to say. "I...um...what are you doing here?"

"A most pleasant room," said Lady Carstairs.

The hero stood up and bowed to her. "With all due respect m'lady, we did not come here to admire the décor." He turned to Joseph. "Sir, we all want to live beyond your imagination. We would all like...a body."

Joseph reeled backwards, his eyes wide with incredulity. "A what?"

"You created us," said Virginia, "you gave us life, but you did not give us substance, and we want to live like normal people."

Joseph looked at the six seated figures. "But, you're alive now."

"Mere shadow, my boy," said the solicitor.

"Ghosts," said the stockbroker.

"I need a real oven for this batter before it spoils," the cook announced.

Joseph swallowed hard. "But...but, how?" Before anyone could answer however, there was a knock at the door and his mother entered. When she looked around the room, Joseph thought that she, or he, or both, would faint.

"Who are you talking to?" she asked.

"I…um…"

"She can't see us. Tell her you were thinking out loud," said the hero helpfully.

"Talking to? Why, nobody. I was just thinking out loud."

"Is that your new book?" Mrs Dawson pointed to the still unopened parcel on the table. "I heard the postman."

"Um…yes."

Mrs Dawson frowned, unable to understand her son's reticence. "Well, may I read it?"

"No point in denying it," said Virginia. "She's your mother, and one way or another, she'll read it."

"I suppose so," said Joseph, but to whom the remark was addressed, was unclear. As he snipped the string and removed the wrapping, rather than elation, he felt ill.

"There is one solution," said the solicitor when Mrs Dawson had departed, "but it's temporary at best. I believe you drew inspiration from the stage. So, turn the book into a play."

"But I'm a novelist, not a playwright, and why do you say it's only temporary?"

"Because when the play closes, we would return to our former selves. Spirits without bodies."

More from desperation than practicality, Joseph said hopefully, "I could always write a third book." One look at their faces told him what he could do with his suggestion.

It was the cook who dealt the final blow. She put the bowl on the table and wiped her hands on her apron. "Right, Mr Dawson – oh yes, we know your real name. Indeed, had you given Mr Astor character, he would have been here as well, but that's beside the point. I need an oven, I need a body, and I need them now. Otherwise, I'll just have to haunt you till I get them."

"As will we all," the hero chipped-in.

"There's an oven in the kitchen," said Joseph timidly. He had completely forgotten about his pseudonym, Giles Astor. Thank goodness he hadn't included a biographical page. "I'm sure my mother won't object if you use it."

"Humph!"

"I think," said the stockbroker standing up, "that Mr Dawson needs time to consider his options, to decide what field to play as it were," and at once, they all vanished.

Joseph slumped into a chair. He had escaped his former difficulties by flight, but not this time, not unless he could conjure up six bodies, and it would take the skill of a great magician to do it. All his pride and delight in the new publication, was gone, replaced by the same misery and despair as before.

His creations however, were far from gone. Joseph was plagued by them, even when he was in bed. Virginia would tickle his nose with a feather just as he was falling asleep. "I want a body," she would say innocently, the double entendre making her giggle.

"Virginia!" Lady Winifred rebuked. "Come away and leave Mr Dawson alone. I am sure he will do his best."

During meals and walks and anywhere else he might venture, Joseph was followed by six invisible shadows, that is to say, invisible to all except himself. One day he said to Virginia, "I never thought things would come to this."

"I am convinced you have a vein of frolicsome devilry, otherwise, I wouldn't be the person I am."

"I do not regret creating you, but one can have too much of a good thing, and there are times when I could do without your presence. You seem to forget that I also created a hero for you."

Virginia waved a hand dismissively. "Oh, he's nice enough, but he can't provide me with a body. Therefore, dear creator, you have my complete devotion until you do."

Joseph groaned, the situation was becoming intolerable, and one evening when he was alone with the stockbroker, he began to protest. "I feel like a prisoner and you are my warders."

The stockbroker, who had been sucking on a smokeless pipe, removed it from his mouth long enough to say, "Now you know how we feel, dear chap. Just as a warder can set someone free, so you can free us."

"But it's impossible. I can't simply fabricate a body."

As before, Joseph's health began to suffer. Finally, as they were sitting down to dinner, his mother said, "What's the matter? I thought you'd be happy with your new book. I liked it far better than the first." Joseph had given her a copy after he'd started work on the second.

"I'm feeling a bit off colour that's all."

"Well, I hope it won't interfere with your appetite. Today we're having your favourite for dinner, roast lamb and mint-sauce." Mrs Dawson paused then said thoughtfully, "I wonder who discovered the combination. Strange how two very different foods work together."

Suddenly, Joseph brought his fist down on the table. All the plates and dishes, 'jumped'. "That's it! That's the answer! Mother, you've done it again."

"Done what dear," she asked, straightening the salt & pepper pots, which had toppled over.

"Excuse me, mother, I need to go to my study." With his heart thumping wildly, Joseph rose from the table and gestured for his shadows to follow. When they were alone he said, "I think I have found a permanent solution, but I must have your word on two counts. Firstly, that you will leave and not disturb me anymore tonight. Secondly, I want you all to meet me at four o'clock tomorrow afternoon, at the Lytton-Under-Lyne, railway station."

"Give us a minute to discuss it," said the solicitor. The shadows huddled in a corner. It took less than 15 seconds. "We agree," he announced.

Grinning like a schoolboy who's lost a bag of marbles but then found a stash of conkers, Joseph returned to the little dining-room. This was one meal he would never forget. "Mother, I'm sorry, but I must return to Lytton tomorrow. I can't explain now, but trust me, everything will be alright."

Straight after dinner, Joseph returned to the now deserted study and wrote six letters. He ran out of the house just in time to catch the last post, and then – oh blessed relief, went for a walk, alone. Now easier in mind and lighter of heart, he returned to the house and went to bed, his sleep completely undisturbed.

Mrs Brown greeted her returning lodger without effusion. "I received your letter," she said tartly. "Your old room is ready."

"I am very glad to see you again," said Joseph, as he, his baggage, and his six shadows, crowded into the narrow hallway.

Mrs Brown shivered. "Hmm…must be a draft. At what time would you like supper?"

"Actually, I am expecting visitors from about seven o'clock onwards." When the landlady's face froze, Joseph quickly added, "Not that I expect you to feed them. It's just that I have business to transact and it will take some time. As a matter of fact, my first piece of business is with you. May we go into the dining-room?" In this instance, the 'we', was collective.

Still with an air of tetchiness, Mrs Brown opened the door and then sat down at the table. "Well?" she prompted, as the shadows arranged themselves around the room, the table not being big enough to accommodate them all.

"Dear Mrs Brown," said Joseph, "I have done you a great wrong. I am now in a position to correct it." He turned to the cook and said, "Slip in and occupy her body."

The cook looked at her own ample girth, and then at the widow's sparse frame. "I'm not sure I like the tenement."

"It's that or nothing, your choice."

"Mr Dawson," said Mrs Brown confusedly, "who are you..." Presto! "I think we'll have fish for supper tomorrow, perhaps with a nice lemon sauce, not too sharp, but not too bland. And you know something else? I have a hankering to bake a cake. Now, where did I put my cookbooks? Oh, that's right, I don't have any. Not to worry, I'll buy some at the market tomorrow. Well, if you would excuse me, sir. I have just enough flour to make a batch of scones," and still babbling about matters culinary, Mrs Brown left the room.

Joseph smiled as he went upstairs to his old room, unpacked, and then bathed, at which function his shadows politely absented themselves. He was just descending the stairs when there was a knock at the front door.

"I'll get it," he called over the clamour of pots & pans. It seemed the 'new' Mrs Brown, was giving her kitchen a thorough inspection. Joseph opened the door. "Ah, good evening Mr Baxter," he said cheerfully, ushering the stiff young man to the dining-room. "You received my letter?"

"Of course," said Baxter languidly, "otherwise I wouldn't have been here."

Joseph wasted neither time nor words. "You cannot do better than animate this feeble creature," he said to the hero.

"What? Him? He's bone idle."

"And you can make a man out of him. Take it or leave it." Presto!

Instantly, Mr Baxter sprang to his feet. "By George, I've just had a brilliant idea. Tomorrow, I shall enlist in the army. It will mean leaving my mother and sisters, but when duty calls only a coward will resist. Nice to see you again, Dawson. I'll send you a note from wherever I'm posted." Such was his enthusiasm, that as he ran out of the house, he cannoned into Mr Hedthrop.

"Watch where you're going," said the magistrate grumpily.

"Sorry," panted Mr Baxter. "Gotta go and save the world," and giving the old reprobate a military salute, he bounded down the street.

Mr Hedthrop was still muttering something about, 'the young bucks of today', when he entered the dining room. "So, Dawson, you have returned. I wonder you have the audacity to show your face around here."

Joseph ignored the terseness and bowed respectfully. "How are you, sir?"

"Below par of course. You and your damned book. I haven't played a round of golf since. Had to content myself with an occasional game of tennis. Silly boring game, there's no skill to it."

Joseph looked meaningfully at the stockbroker. "Your turn."

"Bit 'advanced' isn't he?"

Mr Hedthrop, the colour slowly draining from his face, gaped at Joseph as he spoke to the wall. "True, but he's also a wise old bird, if only he knew how to administer it. What he needs, is your capacity for analysis and logic. Care for the challenge?" Presto!

"Mr Dawson," said Mr Hedthrop, "I understand you have written a new book. I would be greatly interested in discussing it with you. Please, come and dine with me later this week." He checked his fob watch. "Well, I can't sit here gossiping all night, I have court documents to study, and speaking of which, I believe you are about to have another visitor, Mr Swindler."

The latter was indeed approaching the house, and as Joseph watched from behind the curtain, he saw the two men stop and exchange a few words. He could not hear what was said, but it was clear from Mr Swindler's unconcealed expression of alarm, that it was not to his liking. This was reflected when, like months earlier, he stormed into the dining-room.

"Well, Dawson? What do you have to say for yourself? Why did you insist in your letter, that I come here?"

"To restore your dignity and to give you the character you previously lacked."

"Why you impudent…"

"Not quite what I had in mind," said the other solicitor, "but I suppose he'll have to do." Presto!

At once, Mr Swindler stood up and spoke with such conviction, that he might have been addressing the Lord

Chief Justice. "Mr Dawson, I am much pleased that you have returned to Lytton. Though it pains me to say it, since your departure, I have discovered elements of shiftiness and duplicity within my office. I have every desire to correct this, but I need a man I can trust, someone with the strictest integrity. I believe, Mr Dawson, that the man I seek, is you." The room suddenly fell into deep shadow. A small but handsome carriage had just stopped outside the house. "Miss Astoria if I'm not mistaken," said Mr Swindler. "I shall leave you in peace. Call on me tomorrow morning and we will discuss the matter – good night."

"It is most fortunate that I am here," said Lady Winifred. "At least the young lady will be chaperoned, if only in spirit."

Joseph held his breath as Virginia went to the window and saw her 'new' body. Her initial reaction was not encouraging. "She is certainly pretty, but rather inanimate. There is a listlessness in her walk, and she shows not the slightest interest in being here. She reminds me of a doll – one expression, one posture, and stuffed."

"You will change all that," said Joseph gently. Silently he added, "I'm counting on it."

Astoria entered, but did not extend her hand. "Mr Dawson," she said primly, "I thought I made it plain upon our last meeting, that I had no desire to see you again."

"And yet you are here."

"When you wrote to me, pleading that I should visit you this evening, I could do no other. I have no initiative, no power of resistance."

"Fiddlesticks," said Virginia quietly.

Joseph ignored her. "I do hope, Miss Vincent, that the thing you feared has not come to pass."

"What thing?"

"That you have not been claimed by a fortune hunter."

"No. Much to my regret, I have kept very much to myself."

"She means she's peeved because she hasn't been invited to any balls and parties, but she's too polite to say so." Virginia made a most un-lady like growling noise. "Oh, let me at her. I can't stand that kind of 'oh woe is me' type modesty. I'll soon shake-up the county gentry. Goodbye Joseph, and thank you." Presto!

Miss Vincent swayed on her feet, closed her eyes, and clutched at her throat. "Wait," said Lady Winifred, as Joseph made to move forward. "She needs a moment to adjust."

"Goodness me," said Miss Vincent in breathless surprise. All inertia was gone. She stood erect, eyes twinkling, cheeks flushing, and a mischievous smile curling her lips. "I suddenly feel…quite different."

"I am very glad to hear it."

"Why so?" she asked coyly.

"Because you are charming again."

"Thank you, sir," said Astoria, curtsying and laughing at the same time.

Joseph smiled at his 'new' creation. "You are now the embodiment of womanhood, which, if I may be so bold to express it, I strongly admire."

"Fiddlesticks. Men can be so ridiculously obtuse at times. Please, say what you mean."

Having created the character, Joseph knew that Virginia could be exceedingly forthright at times. However, he had not expected to encounter it so soon. He took a deep breath. "Miss Vincent, would you allow me to call on you?"

"Why Mr Dawson," she said coquettishly, "I shall be very disappointed if you do not."

"A fine match I think," said Lady Winifred, as Miss Vincent's carriage pulled away. "Now, what, or should I say 'who', have you in store for me?"

At that moment, there was a firm, almost demanding, knock on the dining-room door, and without waiting for a response, it swung open to admit...the vicar. His clothes were so shabby, that it looked like he'd slept in them for a month. His eyes were vacant, his mouth drooped, and his cheeks were sunken and sallow. The latter were now discernable due to the fact that his once impressive whiskers, were now wispy and limp.

"I am not long for my bed, Mr Dawson," he said mournfully, "so I pray you be expedient."

"I see you have not fared well," said Joseph contritely, for he did indeed feel a measure of guilt. The vicar inclined his head by a fraction. "Happily," Joseph went on, "there is a remedy to hand. You will not be precisely yourself again, but you will certainly be a personality in the parish.

"Now, just a minute," said Lady Winifred indignantly. "This is a man, and therefore by nature, hardly delicate."

"True, but like most men, it's what he needs. As darling Astoria said earlier, men can be ridiculously obtuse. The vicar is a good man, but he needs a gentle guiding hand. Besides, his is the only remaining body."

"In this instance," said Lady Winifred, in one of her renowned flashes of wisdom, "rather than obtuseness, I fear your wits are excessively sharp." She took a step forward, paused, and then said, "Would it be improper if I taught him needle-point?"

Joseph went over and kissed her cheek. Like Mr

Hedthrop earlier, the vicar looked askance at the young man, and thought him, 'quite mad'. "I believe," said Joseph as he led her to the now white-faced clergyman, "that you would never do anything improper." Presto!

In the twinkling of an eye, the vicar's expression altered to one of benign grace, with soft laughter lines about his face. "Bless my soul," he exclaimed, catching sight of his reflection in the mirror above the mantelpiece. "I must visit the barber first thing tomorrow. Hmm…perhaps there is a lesson in this, something about 'revealing one's true self." He walked across to the door, then at the last moment, turned and said absently, "Good night Dawson. Nice to have you back," and still contemplating his next sermon, he quietly left the room.

Mrs Brown popped her head around the door. There was flour on her face, on her hands, and in her hair, yet she had never looked happier. "Excuse me, sir, but are you expecting anyone else?"

"No," said Joseph with a heavy sigh, "not tonight."

"Good, then here's your supper," and she advanced with a steaming dish of mutton stew. "And there's scones for afters," she added, "turned out much better than I expected."

Joseph burst out laughing. "Mrs Brown, you never said truer words."

Three months later, the now much loved vicar, pronounced Joseph and Astoria "Man and wife". Not only did Mrs Brown provide a sumptuous wedding breakfast, but thanks to Mr Chambers, she published several popular cook books.

Mr Baxter served the army with distinction. Unfortunately, a battle injury shortened his service. He returned to Lytton a conquering hero, although the source of the fortune he had accumulated along the way, was fodder for much gossip.

Mr Hedthrop became a highly-respected magistrate, and it was at his suggestion that Mr Swindler offered Joseph a full partnership. He readily accepted, for he had no desire to ever write another book.

Life in Lytton-Under-Lyne, returned to normal. However, there was one peculiarity nobody could explain. Why had the vicar taken to creating in needle-point, pictures of ferrets?

ABOUT THE AUTHOR

Annette Siketa emigrated from England to Australia with her mother in 1974. She was diagnosed with severe breast cancer on September 11th, 2001, (THE September 11th), and was told she would not live beyond Christmas. Seven years later, a routine eye operation tragically rendered her blind. Her life then changed dramatically, and it was her penchant for creating imaginative stories that 'saved' her, though at the time, she knew nothing about professional writing. From a technical standpoint, her first novel, *The Dolls House*, was an unmitigated disaster. However, she persevered and learned the craft, and has now written a wide variety of award-winning short stories and novels, including *Double Take*, and, *The Ghosts of Camals College*.

Alfie Dog Fiction

Taking your imagination for a walk

For hundreds of short stories, collections
and novels visit our website at
www.alfiedog.com

Join us on Facebook
http://www.facebook.com/AlfieDogLimited

33929960R00097

Made in the USA
Charleston, SC
27 September 2014